Storks

This book is dedicated to the unique group of women who refused to play a conventional woman's role in a country at war.

I hope that through this work of fiction more people will
become aware of the reality.

Chapter One
A tomboy, a toff and a yank

Maggie looked down at the world below; unaware of how it was about to change her world forever.

She landed the small biplane perfectly, as usual. The tiny German airfield wasn't as quiet as it normally was. A group of very eager looking men were gathered around a set of building plans spread over the bonnet of a large black Mercedes-Benz parked next to the small, dilapidated, control tower. Two of the men were displaying their politics on their sleeves in the form of swastika armbands.

She climbed down from the cockpit and walked across the airfield. Her shock of red hair fell to her shoulders as she removed her flying helmet, causing a somewhat dramatic interruption to the, until then, preoccupied men. Joseph Büchner, a thin, small man in his late fifties, wearing a mechanics overall that looked about the same age as he was, greeted her.

"What kept you?" said Joseph

"Filling in about four hundred forms." Replied Maggie.

"What, just for a few spares?" said Joseph.

"Yes and they still didn't give me all of them.

A look of puzzlement came across Joseph's face

"Why?" He asked,

"Just to be bloody awkward I suppose.

"Replied Maggie.

Joseph took the metal box of spares from Maggie as they walked together towards a small cottage on the edge of the airfield.

"It's getting so difficult." Said Joseph.

Maggie glanced back at the group of men and commented. "Who are that lot?"

"They are looking at making a few changes to the airfield." Replied Joseph.

"Not with your consent, I take it?" said Maggie.

"You don't argue Maggie…not with those people.

Maggie took another look back at the group of unwanted visitors who seemed to be more interested in striking a pose than the business in hand.

"Look on the bright side," said Maggie, "they may just build us a nice new concrete runway."

"I think the Luftwaffe will have priority if they do mein liebling."

Three hundred and fifty miles away in the heart of the southeast English countryside Dianna and Rodger Bamford, a very distinguished late middle age couple were having afternoon tea on a vast and very manicured lawn, sweeping down to an idyllic lake.

The peace and quite was disturbed by the sound of a light aeroplane above them. Dianna took off her wide brimmed summer straw hat and looked up somewhat excited.

"Oh look Rodger, isn't that Joy?"

Without looking at the aeroplane he continued to read his paper as he answered in a somewhat despondent tone. "Yes darling, that is your daughter. Notice I say <u>your</u> daughter. With the complaints I've had from the locals, who have things like livestock to consider, it's safer to deny my parenthood.

Without paying too much attention to Rodger's comment Dianne continued.

"She's doing awfully well to say that she only learnt to fly a few months ago."

"That's what you said when she took up motorcycling moments before she destroyed the summer house." Said Rodger.

Diana just smiled as she watched her daughter and said, with a touch of envy in her voice," looks such fun."

Roger finally looked up at the plane and then at Diana as he commented.

"Mmm, obvious where she gets it from."

A few miles away, and out of sight of Diana and Roger, an old farmer rushed to herd his sheep out of the way of the light plane as it silently made an approach to land in a small meadow.

"Lie down girls," he shouted to his two dogs, "you don't want that propeller thing up your arse."

The dogs yapped and ran around in circles, not knowing whether to herd the unfamiliar contraption or attack it. This was never in their long and intensive sheepdog training. The plane bounced a couple of times and came to a halt.

Joy, a slim, attractive girl with a wild mane of blond hair and a constant wide-eyed expression, as if every second of life was a totally new experience, climbed out of the cockpit. She shouted to the farmer in a mistress to servant type manner. "Won't be long, keep the dogs back, there's a good chap. Don't want them peeing on the tyres." Her passenger, or more like latest victim, followed her - a ginger haired, nervous looking young man called Jimmy. "Do you usually land here?" asked Jimmy with a slight tremor in his voice.

"Only when the engine fails." Replied Joy, now pulling a rubber hose from the engine. Jimmy turned his back to Joy, lent on the lower wing of the biplane and was violently sick. The old farmer, completely engrossed in the proceedings, took a spontaneous step back to avoid being decorated by Jimmy's previous lunch. "Oh dear Jimmy, did something not agree with you? Asked Joy. "Don't worry there's just a bit of dirt in the fuel line. I'll soon have it cleared and we'll be on our way again."

"Oh God," muttered Jimmy as he was sick again, causing the farmer to take a further step back.

A large wooden propeller, covered in signatures, adorned a wall in Joseph's and his wife Maria's small dining room. A kind of shrine to like minded men who, for reasons only known to themselves and bemused by many, had a passion for leaving the ground in various and often precarious aircraft.

Seated around an old Bavarian hand-carved table the German couple, dressed very traditionally, were fussing over Maggie, now looking almost feminine in a light summer rose print dress, a poor attempt at makeup and looking as if she wouldn't know one end of an airplane from the other. She finished her last

spoonful of dessert and sat back in her chair.
"That was your best strudel ever Maria." Said Maggie.

Maria's chubby cheeks blushed a little as she took Maggie's empty plate and walked towards the kitchen, talking as she went.
"Which means you would like some more."
"Damn clever you Germans." Said Maggie.
Joseph walked over to a glass cabinet and took out two crystal glasses and held them up to a small corner table light to check if they were as sparkling as they should have been. Maggie responded to the ritual by taking a bottle of schnapps from a large antique pine dresser displaying generations of porcelain and glass. Enjoying the moment with his two favourite women, Joseph smiled saying.
"Maria has always wanted a daughter."

Maggie came back with an instant reply as she poured the drinks.

"And you've always wanted a son. And with me around you've got both right?" Joseph held up his glass and announced a toast.

"And the best son and daughter we could wish for."

Maggie answered the toast with another.

"And both of me promise to look after you when you're both old and doddery."

Joseph's expression changed to one of concern as he looked into his glass. Maggie ran her finger round the rim of her glass. Their timing was synchronised as, after a few seconds, they both looked up and into each other's eyes.

Maggie spoke first. "I think I've just hit on the real reason for this wonderful dinner."

"Maggie you must leave." Said Joseph.

"I haven't had my second piece of strudel yet." Said Maggie desperately trying to make light of the situation.

"Maggie for god's sake let me be serious." Snapped Joseph as he glared at Maggie and then stared into his glass.

"So it really is a farewell dinner." Replied Maggie trying to get eye contact with Joseph. Becoming aware of Maggie's sudden feeling of abandonment Joseph pulled his chair closer to her and continued in a softer tone.

"It's getting too dangerous for you here, people are being arrested if they've even visited England and you're English and flying over things that they are trying to hide everyday."

"I know you're right Joseph." Replied Maggie. "But I thought if I ignored it, it might just go away."

"Look, if you won't think of yourself" said Joseph, "think of how Maria and I would feel if anything happened to you."

"Like what?" said Maggie causing Joseph to get angry again.

"A conveniently arranged accident for instance. Lost in bad weather or a sudden mid-air explosion. Maggie I'm not trying to frighten you but these things happen."

Maria entered the room with an extra large helping of strudel. She placed it in front of Maggie and clasped her hand with affection. She obviously heard the last part of the conversation between Joseph and Maggie. Maggie looked up and smiled. The three of them carried on as if nothing had been said. Joseph turned to Maggie and said quietly "Maggie?" she poured him another schnapps as she reassured him.

"Yes OK." Joseph smiled and said. "If you eat much more you'll need a bigger engine to get you off the ground." Maggie blew out her cheeks to imitate a fatter version of herself. "I'm working on becoming a barrage balloon."

The knock on the door disturbed the laughter. Maria got up to answer it leaving Joseph and Maggie both attacking the last piece of strudel with spoons while making the sound of diving aeroplanes.

Maria re-entered nervously. Following closely behind was a tall, gaunt looking man wearing a leather Gestapo issue coat, which made a kind of creaking sound as the man moved, adding to the threat that now filled the room. Without any introduction he spoke in a cold clipped tone.

"Fräulein Stewart?"

Maggie glanced towards Joseph and Maria realising their concern.

"Yes." Maggie answered. The intruder continued.

"I am to escort you to Berlin where you will leave Germany for Switzerland."

Maggie stood to face the man and questioned.

"What?"

Without acknowledging Maggie's question he continued.

"When in Switzerland you will be met by a British representative who will arrange your deportation to England. We will leave now."

Maggie, just at the point of exploding, noticed how worried Maria had become as she held Joseph's hand. Maggie glanced down to see Maria's legs shaking uncontrollably.

"Can I pick up some things first?" said Maggie. "Everything will be sent on to you after it has been cleared. I will see you outside. You have one minute." He turned to Joseph, raised his arm and snapped, "Heil Hitler." He left as impolitely as he arrived.

Maggie, Maria and Joseph were silent for a few seconds overpowered by an atmosphere that seemed like death itself. "I'll write to you," said Maggie desperately trying to break the silence.

"The letters will never get through," said Joseph "don't worry we will be fine" "How do you know?" said Maggie in an almost childlike voice.

"They've got what they want, my airfield…and now you."

Maria burst into tears causing Maggie to, somewhat symbolically, knock one of the crystal glasses of celebration off the table as she rushed to throw her arms around Maria. She didn't even notice that a small piece of broken glass had made a tiny cut on her ankle.

"Take care…please." Said Joseph fighting to hold back the tears himself.

Maggie left. She looked back to see Maria still crying and Joseph with eyes closed shaking his head. Maggie couldn't help thinking that this was the last image she would ever have of them.

Outside, the Gestapo agent extinguished a cigarette with his foot as he opened the door of the black staff car for Maggie to get in. She sat in the centre of the dark leather seat biting her lip to stop it trembling as the Nazi representative closed the door on part of Maggie's life.

"Anyone seen my ugly sister?" The American accent of Bob Kletzki, a dark haired and very handsome man in his early twenties, contrasted with the typically British setting of the Cambridge University playing fields on a warm summer afternoon. A male student with foppish blonde hair, wearing a cricket jumper tied around his neck answered as he pointed to a corner of the field.
"Left at the cricket nets old man, deep in study as usual." As Bob strode off across the

field, he acknowledged a small group of female students sitting astride their bicycles talking and laughing. One of the girls gave a wiggly-fingered little wave. A voice with a strong East European accent disturbed Bob's thoughts.

"Hey fancy half an hours practice with Poland's greatest cricketer?" Romek Janowski ran alongside Bob, desperately trying to keep up, wearing cricket pads and carrying a bat. His quite skinny build made the pads strapped around his legs look enormous.

"No thanks Romek, that game makes me fall asleep. The day they take on cheerleaders is the day I may consider taking up cricket." Said Bob.

Bob looked over Romek's shoulder to catch sight of a female student just clearing a high jump. As she brushed sand from her legs she looked up towards Bob and smiled. Romek noticed the exchange saying,

"You know I've often wondered, if my parents had emigrated from Poland to the United States when yours did, would I have become a smooth talking American that the whole female population of Cambridge is in love with?" Bob, still looking towards the young high jumper answered,

"It's not nationality it's personality. You've either got it…or you play cricket. See ya later." Connie was everything opposite to the "ugly sister" that Bob had asked after. Raven wavy hair, huge eyes and a Rita Hayworth mouth. She was petite and looked even smaller curled up on the grass with her nose in a book.

"What's a scruffy little kid doing in a beautiful place like this?" said Bob as he approached her.

"What do you want? Can't you find an English girl to darn your socks? Answered Connie.

"Don't be crazy they're standing in line" said Bob. He took a letter out of his pocket and handed it to his sister.

"You've got a letter from Mom and Dad."

"Dad still saving money on the postage then" said Connie. "Last time I got your letter in mine."

"He needs to with these fees", said Bob.

As Connie began to read her letter Bob picked up the book that she'd been reading. It said on the cover, "Principles of Flight"

"And he wouldn't be too happy with what you've been studying."

"It's your fault, remember?" said Connie.

"OK so I took you up once, most girls are terrified." Bob argued.

Connie looked up from reading her letter.

"I'm not most girls, even though your flying is enough to terrify anyone."

"So it's my fault that you joined the University Air Squadron, god knows why they let you in. When are you flying next?" asked Bob.

"Today if the weather holds." Getting a little over excited," Connie continued.

"By the way when you do a flick roll how far do you pull the stick back before you give it full rudder?"

Bob put the book down and snapped back at Connie showing a fair bit of brotherly concern.
"You don't want to go doing that sort of thing on your own, you could black out."

A little smirk on Connie's face made Bob realise that he'd slightly blown his cool image. He quickly noticed an attractive girl playing hockey and changed the subject.
"Hey who's that? She's cute."
Connie attempted, what she thought was, a typical English accent.
"She's terribly wich, has a soooper chap at Sandhurst and you don't stand a chance you vulgar American."

The playfulness was interrupted by the sound of an airplanc high above them; they both gazed upward in a shared longing to be flying the small craft doing some graceful and very accomplished aerobatics. Without taking her eyes off it Connie asked.

"Oh wow, what a honey. What is it Bob?"

"It's called a Bulldog," answered Bob, "Beautiful isn't it? I know the guy who owns it so I could take you up if you'd like?"

For a brief moment Connie thought that Bob was answering her but as she looked in his direction she realised that the young attractive hockey player had wondered over and Bob had his arm around her shoulder pointing towards the biplane.

Connie smiled to herself, gathered up her things and got up to leave.

"Looks like I've just become the number three that makes a crowd. Bye big brother." She turned to the wide-eyed hockey player as she left.

"Don't settle for anything less than champagne and three courses, he's loaded."

"Thanks sis, I owe you a large one." Said Bob cynically. "And remember what I said about flick rolls."

As Connie strolled across the university playing field her thoughts journeyed back to June 2nd 1923, her third birthday. The big day had arrived at last. She sat up, in bed in her tiny room above her parents grocery store in Brooklyn New York, having not slept much at all the night before due to the excitement of becoming the owner of a brand new Flapper Doll that she'd been hinting about for months.

Eventually Mom and Dad pushed open her door. "Happy birthday darling," they said in strong Polish accents. Even back then, with their minds firmly set on success in America, they insisted on speaking English. Six-year-old Bob shuffled in after them in pajamas about three sizes too big for him. "We've got you something little princess. It's not much but soon when we're rich you can have whatever your heart desires." Said dad as he handed her what was obviously not the Flapper Doll.

Little Connie looked confused as she slowly opened the first present, a chocolate bar from the grocery store. The second present wrapped in brown paper, also from the store, was all but doll-shaped. Her tiny hands pulled off the string and ripped open the paper to reveal a book of Grimm's' Fairy Tales, obviously second hand by the state of the battered edges. Connie just stared at the front cover and without looking up said, "thank you."

Dad smiled as he pushed Mom towards the door. "Now you enjoy your lovely new book while Mamma and me open the store." As soon as they left tears rolled down her cheeks as she sat motionless on her bed. Bob shared her silence for a few seconds before speaking very softly to the little sister who he normally teased constantly.

"Don't cry Con I'm going to get you something you'll love…I won't be long."

As Bob left the room Connie felt that her whole world had fallen apart. She would never get to unwrap that big-eyed doll, change her clothes, pretend she was its best friend and have hours of little girl adventures together. The waiting and excitement was all over. She sobbed as quietly as she possibly could not to draw attention to her disappointment.

A few minutes past before Bob stood in the doorway again. He had his hands behind his back. "Got it Con, here you are…careful it might still be a bit wet."
From behind his back Bob produced his treasured and favourite wooden model areoplane that he'd just painted pink. "I've changed it into a girls present and it's all yours to keep." Connie smiled to herself as

she pushed open the door of the university lodgings.

A thought occurred to her that she had never said thank you all those years ago.

She whispered softly, "Thanks Bob."

Chapter two
New recruits

A military policeman lifted the barrier to let a staff car leave a large airfield in southeast England. Inside the car were two senior

ranking RAF officers. Both were pretty unhappy and one was decidedly grumpy. He muttered to himself as he thumbed through a classified report. Frustration quickly got the better of him as he expressed an opinion.
"The last time I saw something as idiotic as this was when I was watching the local Home Guard doing drill practice with pitch forks and broom handles."

The second officer didn't disagree but was a little more rational.
"I know it's not ideal but beggars can't be choosers right now. We need all the pilots we can get." The first officer threw the report onto the seat of the car and continued.
"But they're women for heavens sake, they'll be more concerned with adjusting their stocking seams than their fuel mixture."

The second officer replied, "It's not as though they're going into combat…they are only delivering the aircraft to the squadrons."

"And they are only flying those aircraft. Doesn't anyone realise what a Spitfire costs?" Barked the first officer.

Unable to comment further, the second officer glanced out of the window as the staff car made its way through the twisting country lanes.

At another airfield to the west of London a small crowded hut, full of mainly women, were being addressed by a poe-faced looking small man in an Air Transport Auxiliary uniform. "You may not realise it but today you are making history. You are about to become as important as any fighting service that this country has…" He paused to give his speech maximum effect…"God 'elp us."

Maggie who was sitting at the back of the room cringed at the remark.
"What a terribly unpleasant man," said Joy who was sitting next to Maggie.
"My names Joy, what's yours?" Maggie a little taken aback by Joy's very aristocratic accent answered,
"Maggie."

Noticing the introductions going on at the back of the room the officious little man shouted, "If you two ladies could talk about your knitting patterns some other time I'll get on with the briefing." Maggie muttered under her breath, "Bastard!"

She hears another voice on the other side of her comment,

"Asshole!"

Maggie looked in the direction of the voice to see Connie. The three women looked at each other and smiled.

Maggie and Connie both noticed the wide-eyed look of excitement on Joy's face and gave each other a puzzled smile.

Sometime later, after being subjected to a few more sexist insults and a lot of taking notes on the procedure of delivering aircraft to the operational squadrons all over England, the newly acquainted threesome were in the airfield canteen with mugs of tea. Joy was looking at hers rather curiously, a little different to the delicate bone china that she was used to.

The conversation had got around to revealing their individual backgrounds.

"Dad was born and brought up in Poland, then came over to Brooklyn to seek his fortune," said Connie. "I think if he hadn't had Mom with him he would never have made it. He's got a bit of an ego problem when it comes to being nice to people. So Mom got on with the business side while Dad got on with the manual work"

"And how did you end up over here?" asked Maggie.

"I suppose my brother and I are another side to Dad's ego. To have your kids go to Cambridge is great for the neighbours. We went along with it because despite how I'm making him sound, he really is a great guy and deserves to feel proud."

Connie caught sight of both girls smiling and confessed,

"Oops, sorry that sounded like a speech."

"And a pretty good one," said Maggie. "So was he a flyer?" she continued.

"No not at all, closest he ever got to taking to the air was wearing thick socks in the winter in the early days of his fruit and veg store. My brother Bob had the bug since he was a kid and I caught it a couple of years ago when he took me up to show me the English countryside. I was more interested in flying than the view. And I suppose there was an element of little sister wanting to beat big brother at his own game." Said Connie.

"What's your brother doing now?" asked Maggie.

"He's become very moral lately, which is very unlike him." Answered Connie. "He's re-claimed his roots, joined the RAF and is flying with a Polish fighter squadron out of a place called North Weald."

"You sound a bit cynical." Questioned Maggie.

"I suppose it's just my way of being as worried as hell about him." Said Connie.

After a moment's pause and nervous fiddling with a glass salt pot, Joy tried to offer a little comfort.

"Oh I'm sure he'll be fine." Connie smiled at Joy thankfully and changed the subject.

"So when did you two tuck your frocks in your knickers and take to the air?"

At a, strictly men only, table next to theirs the man who previously gave the briefing gave Connie a disapproving look. An older friendlier looking man smiled to himself.

"Mine's a bit of a long story", said Maggie "My Dad was an aircraft fitter in The Royal Flying Corps, then he went to de Havilland in the 20's. My mother died when I was a kid so he had to cope with me as well as work. We used to live in a little place on the airfield where he worked. I used to help him when I wasn't at school, which was quite often. Where most kids had pet kittens and dolls, I had a set of socket spanners. So airplanes were always part of my life whether I liked it or not, fortunately I loved it. The flying started when I was about twelve. A friend of Dad's called Joseph was a German pilot who was a prisoner of war in England from 1916. After the war he brought his wife Maria over and decided to settle. Dad was always good to him and got him a job at the airfield. In return they both took pity on both of us. Maria would cook for us and help with the housework.

Connie interrupted,
"Wow, so you've got German friends." The next table heard the remark and all looked across at the women. Connie realised her faux pas and apologised, "oops sorry, excuse the loud mouthed American."
"Don't worry about it", said Maggie. "But yes you're right I'm very fond of them. Joseph taught me to fly and he and his wife Maria took me in because my Dad died of cancer. Then Joseph inherited a bit of land in

Germany, so we packed our bags and turned that plot of land into a thriving little air freight business." Maggie's voice cracked a little as the memories come flooding back. She forced a smile to finish her story. "And all was wonderful 'till Mr. bloody Hitler goosed stepped into our lives."

"It must be so hard to help fight the cause against what has become, like your home and family." Said Connie.
"It's also very difficult for Joseph and Maria. Being very loyal Germans they don't exactly want to lose the war but they don't want Hitler's mob to win it either. Imagine that for a predicament?" Said Maggie.
"Shit what a nightmare", was all Connie could think of saying.

"So come on Joy", continued Connie. "What's your story?"

"Daddy bought me a plane for my birthday." Said Joy perfectly innocently.

Maggie and Connie both lent forward in anticipation of the rest of the story. Joy just took a sip of her tea.

"Yes and?" Questioned Connie.

"That's it really." Said Joy.

"How did you end up here in the ATA?" asked Maggie.

"It sounded like fun." Replied Joy.

Maggie and Connie looked at each other in complete disbelief. Joy smiled back completely confident with her explanation. Realising that they're weren't gong to get any further with this one Maggie said, "Well this won't get the mangle cranked."

"And I've got a train to catch. Are you coming Joy?" Said Connie.

"No I'm getting a lift thanks." Answered Joy.

Maggie and Connie got up to leave as Joy gazed out of the window still sipping her tea as if it was something of a novelty. As they left the canteen a Rolls Royce pulled up, driven by a grumpy looking chauffeur in full livery. Maggie and Connie looked at each other.

"You don't think?" Asked Maggie.

"Yes I do." Answered Connie. "Guess that's how the other half live.

"And it looks like we're going to have to live with it." Said Maggie.

Ernest, the chauffeur got out of the car and gazed around muttering to himself.

"Bloody dump, where the 'ell is she?"

"She's in there." Said Connie anticipating that it was Joy he was looking for.

"Bloody 'ell" remarked Ernest as he pushed open the door to the canteen.

"Well I think we're going to have a ball." Said Connie as she slung the strap of her gas mask over her shoulder.

"Not sure about a ball but I'm thinking it will be something of an education, especially for our posh friend in there," replied Maggie.

"Can't wait." Said Connie, "See you next week."

Chapter three
To a Skylark

Bob tugged on his harness to check it was properly locked as he taxied the Hurricane for take off. The squadron of nine fighters rose to the air and banked to the left towards the coast. Squadron Leader Tom Marsden's voice cut through the roar of the engines on the pilot's intercoms.

"You'll be pleased to know that you may see your first bit of action today children, so keep tight and no chatting unless it's essential."

Excited Polish voices where heard in response.

"I o czasie też."

"Jest dla Polski"

"Pierwszy trzy są mój"

"And keep it in English!" Barked Marsden.

Bob smiled at the exchange. He clipped on his oxygen mask and looked out of his canopy at three of the other Hurricanes hanging, as if, motionless in the sky beside him. He systematically scanned the clear sky for German fighters. His experience as a pilot and his intense, albeit condensed, combat training gave him a sense of self- confidence. He was longing to prove himself worthy of the uniform that he was so proud to be wearing. He had become one of the knights of the air that the schoolboys constantly talked about and the girls that he adored fell at his feet for.

In one of the other cockpits a nineteen-year-old pilot was nervously checking his instrument panel as if he was still at flying school. He eventually became a little more relaxed, dropped his shoulders and eased his grip on the control column.
The few seconds of calm were suddenly, completely contrasted by a frenzy of splintering wood, tearing fabric and shattering

glass. Hardly any sound accompanied the visual turmoil that ensued. The young pilot froze. Locked in fear he was only able to move his eyes as he looked down at blood pouring from his legs and side. His body then went into uncontrollable spasm. Panicking Polish voices from the other pilots broke the silence as more holes ripped into the young man's flying suit causing his own flesh to spit back at him. His chin dropped onto his chest moments before the explosion obliterated both man and machine.

Watching in horror at the remaining, descending fragments Bob was suddenly distracted as the invisible enemy dealt a fatal blow to another unsuspecting pilot.
He starred at the charred, burnt body hanging motionless in the parachute straps just a few

yards from him. Barely resembling the pilot that he knew, miraculously able to get out of his Hurricane but unable to survive the fireball that he had left behind.

Bob's first battle had lasted about one minute with no opportunity to retaliate.

Little reassurance came from Marsden as he announced. "Now you know what life is really like up here. That's what the school boys, who are longing to enlist, don't see as they come out of their choir practice and look up at the brave pilots."

The remaining fighters, in varying states of damage, landed. Some precariously, like battered boxers leaving the ring. Bob brought his aircraft to a halt and sat motionless gazing up to the sky. He saw Marsden walk past him and slid back his canopy climbed out and ran to catch up with him as he headed for the briefing room.

"Where the fuck did they come from?" Shouted Bob.

"From behind and above." Replied Marsden still looking straight ahead.

"How many were there?" Continued Bob.

"Three" answered Marsden.

"Three?" Shouted Bob in disbelief.

"Yes three, flight sergeant. Three very experienced one o nine pilots beating the crap out of a whole squadron of rookies and pissing off."

Shocked and speechless Bob stood still as Marsden carried on walking without looking back.

A week later, on the outskirts of Cambridge, Connie boarded a bus while the driver struggled to lift her old, battered brown leather suitcase onto the luggage rack. She settled into her seat and looked out of the window as the sand coloured university buildings gave way to country lanes and farm buildings. She took a letter from her pocket. It was from Bob and was, at least, the third time she had read it.

"Dear Con, We saw our first bit of action yesterday. If that's how it's going to be then this whole thing will be a breeze. One guy got a little shot up but nothing serious. He probably wasn't paying attention. Those German pilots aren't what they're cracked up to be. Remember old Romek? Well he's doing his bit in the war office. He always was a bright boy. Cambridge seems like a hundred years ago these days.

Last week I was browsing through a few of my old books and came across this Wordsworth poem. It seems to be pretty apt for both of us, so I thought you might like it."

Connie unfolded the enclosed page that Bob had torn out from a book of poetry and imagined hearing her brother's voice as she read it.

To a Skylark
Up with me! up with me into the clouds!
For thy song, Lark, is strong;
Up with me, up with me into the clouds!
Singing, singing,
With clouds and sky about thee ringing,
Lift me, guide me till I find

That spot which seems so to thy mind!"

She smiled as she carefully folded it, put it back into the envelope and finished reading Bob's letter.
"Take care sis and no flick rolls."

The reassurance of Bob being safe combined with gazing at hedgerows and wheat fields must have caused her to doze off. She woke suddenly as she heard the bus driver calling.
"We're here Miss, White Waltham"
Connie realised that Bob's letter was still on her lap. She quickly put it in pocket, grabbed her coat and collected her bag outside the bus. Maggie, who was waiting for her at the airfield gates, wasted no time in coming straight to the point.

"We're in rabbit hutch twenty seven, over there."

Connie wasn't really listening. A small biplane that had just landed on the far corner of the airfield had distracted her.

"Looks like the landed gentry has just landed." She said.

"Nothing like arriving in style," said Maggie.

Joy climbed out from the small plane and came rushing over to join the other two.

"It's absolutely beautiful up there today." She said.

Together they walked towards a row of small wooded huts.

Joys skipped along beside Connie and Maggie like a puppy on its first walk "Won't be long before we're in Spitfires girls."

"I think they might give us something a little less expensive first." Answered Maggie.
Connie joined in with the excitement as she pulled an old box camera from her shoulder bag.
"I'm going to take a picture of everything that I get to fly."

Hut twenty seven eventually came into view, as did Ernest, leaning on the door of the Rolls Royce with a stack of suitcases on the roof of the car. He had obviously gone ahead with the luggage.
Joy announced, "Come and meet Ernest."
Connie silently mouthed the word "Ernest" to Maggie who had to look away for fear of laughing.
"Ernest, meet Maggie and Connie my new friends."

"Any friend of Miss Joy usually ends up as a problem for me," muttered Ernest as he started to take the suitcases off the roof.
Maggie whispered to Connie, "miserable sod."
"I kinda like him." Connie whispered back.

Looking at the tiny hut, about to be occupied by the three unlikely room mates, Maggie said, "Well it's not much but it's home."
"Do you mind if I just think of it as not much?" replied Connie.
"I think it's rather sweet, I've always wanted to rough it." Said Joy emphasising the words "Rough it" as if it was an exciting new adventure.
"You do know there's no maid service?" said Maggie

"Never mind I'm sure we'll…oh you're pulling my leg aren't you?" laughed Joy.

Ernest appeared from inside the hut to collect the next lot of Joy's bags saying.
"Due to the size of the accommodation, do you want me to take a few of the suitcases back or build you an extra wing Miss Joy?"

"Oh shut up Ernest." Snapped Joy as she barged past Ernest followed by Maggie and Connie who gave Ernest a sympathetic glance.

"Where's the bathroom Maggie?" asked Joy. Maggie held open a door to reveal a tin bath, a toilet and washbasin, all crammed into a tiny room with one high window.
"In here." Said Maggie.

"Oh how tiny, where's <u>your</u> bathroom?" Said Joy naively.

Maggie continued to hold open the door. "In here."

Joy squeezed past Maggie to go into the small room, asking as she went.

"Oh we're sharing then, where's Connie's bathroom?"

"In there." Shouted Maggie starting to lose her patience.

"Well I suppose we could have a rota." Answered Joy just before she gave out a loud shriek.

"Ernest, there's a spider in here!"

"'Ope it's a big un," muttered Ernest.

Connie turned to Ernest and said, "Think she's going to find it difficult?"

"I do 'ope so, it'll do her good. This is the 'appiest day of my life" Answered Ernest as he went into the bathroom passing Joy who was rushing out.

"Wouldn't like to be around when he's not happy then," whispered Maggie to Connie.

From outside the tiny bathroom they could hear Earnest talking to, what could have only been, the spider. "Come on little fella, you don't want to be staying in here, shrieking like that will make you go deaf."

Earnest reemerged carefully transporting the spider in both hands to a safer location.
He turned to Joy, who backed off at the thought of what he was carrying.
"If there's nothing else I'll be off."
"Yes, yes, go, go," said Joy, waving Earnest past with both hands.

His parting comment was directed at Connie and Maggie, "Good luck you two."

Chapter four
In at the deep end

Fishwick was sitting bolt upright at his immaculately tidy desk rearranging a few papers. He was in his late forties and judging by the medal ribbons displayed on his Air Transport Auxiliary uniform was a veteran of the First World War. He was small in stature with a round face, slightly off-centre parting and thin moustache on an equally thin lip. A knock on the door caused a short and sharp reply.

"In"

Maggie, Connie and Joy entered. Fishwick wasted no time in dominating the moment. Without moving his head, he raised his eyes to them and said,

"Good morning ladies. My name is Fishwick. The nicknames range from Fishface to Codpiece, so if you would like to pick one now we can get on with the business in hand." There followed a slight pause as the three women looked at each other, not quite knowing how to respond to the unusual introduction. Fishwick again took the lead and continued.

"No?...you do disappoint me but it's early days yet. Do let me know when you think of one, it's always highly amusing. In the meantime I have your assignments. Whose Stewart?"

Maggie stepped forward and answered.

"Er, me sir."

"As you're the most experienced pilot you'll be delivering an Anson to White Waltham from Preston. It's a twin engine…"

To Fishwick's somewhat surprise Maggie butted in.

"Yes I know I've flown one before."

"Good," replied Fishwick. "But you are still required to read the pilot's handling notes."

He pushed a small instruction manual towards her. At the same time he handed another couple of similar documents to Connie and

Joy saying, "You two will be taking two Tiger Moths from here to Brize Norton."

"Tiger Moths?" Questioned Joy. "We can fly those with our eyes closed. When are we getting Spitfires?"

Maggie and Connie cringed as Fishwick, without getting the slightest bit ruffled, replied.

"You'll deliver a Spitfire when I think you are ready, which could mean you'll never deliver a Spitfire. And as far as the Tiger Moths are concerned you will not fly them with your eyes closed. Please collect your train fare back from the cashier. Good day ladies."

Not seeing a whole big enough to be swallowed up in, Maggie and Connie smiled sweetly and shuffled out of the door. Joy followed them slamming the door behind her.

"Well as far as I'm concerned he's talked himself into his own nickname." Said Joy getting a little red in the face.

Maggie and Connie looked at each other waiting for the name to be revealed.

"Mackerel!" said Joy

"Why Mackerel in particular?" Questioned Maggie.

Joy stomped off like a punished child answering the question as she went.

"It always makes me sick."

Connie and Maggie burst into laughter.

"Don't you just love her?" Said Connie.

"If I must." Said Maggie.

"Well I guess I'll see you later." Said Connie.

"Have a good trip. Snapshot number one

coming up." She pulled her camera from her pocket and hurried off after Joy.

A couple of mechanics were sitting on wooden crates watching Connie and Joy walk towards the Tiger Moths. They were a slimy looking pair. One had a few years and pounds on the other and looked even more devious by experience. He wiped his hands on an oily handkerchief and commented.
"Well what have we here?"
"A couple of crackers by the look of things." Answered the younger mechanic.
"Wrong," said the older man. "What we have here, are two pilots in need of instruction…and of course our experience."
He gave his younger workmate a sickly smile. It eventually dawned on the younger man.
"Oh right."

The older man got up saying, "You take the blonde and I'll teach the brunette a thing or two."

As Connie and Joy arrived at the Tiger Moths they were still talking about the encounter with Fishwick.
"You probably just upset him about the Spitfire thing. I'm sure he's a decent guy really." Said Connie.
"If he'd spoken to a man like that," grumbled Joy, " Fishwick would have had his chips."
"I think I prefer your mackerel joke." Said Connie.

As they both started to look over the Tiger Moths the two mechanics arrived on the scene.

"Good morning ladies. Do you have your papers please?" said the older one.

"Sure, here you go." Said Connie.

The mechanic merely glanced over the papers and continued, "American accent if I'm not mistaken maam? Glad to have you on board. Your orders are in order, as they say. So after a little personal instruction you can be on your way."

The mechanic handed back the papers and put his other hand on Connie's shoulder. Connie looked at his hand coldly and glanced across at Joy who was getting chatted up by the other mechanic.

"That won't be necessary," said Connie, "we're both familiar with Tiger Moths."

"That is as maybe," replied the mechanic, "but we've got our jobs to think of see. Rules is rules – won't take long and who knows…you might even learn a thing or two."

Connie's eyes narrowed as she stepped onto the lower wing of the biplane and felt the mechanics hands around her waist in a pathetic attempt to help her up. Joy sat frozen in her seat as the other mechanic's hand brushed against her breasts as he checked her harness. The older mechanic pulled the airplane's control column back between Connie's legs in an excuse for showing her the controls. "Seen a few joysticks in your time I'd bet? Experienced young lady like you, 'specially being from the land of the free, if you know what I mean?'
She slid upwards in her seat.
Connie glanced over to Joy to see her suffering similar humiliation.

The younger mechanics face was now pressed up against Joy's as he pointed into the far distance to give her runway instructions.
"Now don't forget to keep to the west taxiway and remember to avoid the cesspit just before the runway threshold. Don't want you lovely ladies smelling of anything other than roses now do we?"

After taking further liberties and making more innuendo comments the two mechanics walked slowly back towards their hanger laughing.
"A few more like that and it'll make this job a lot more worthwhile and the war a lot more bearable." Said the older mechanic.

Suddenly the roar of the Tiger Moth's engines interrupted the men's swaggering walk. With their tails lifted off the ground the planes were speeding towards the men the propellers aimed straight at them.

The Tiger Moths skillfully herded the mechanics like sheep. Connie's plane blocked the entrance, and the men's sanctuary, of the hanger while Joy forced them to head off across the airfield. After an entertaining few minutes for the women workers at the airfield, who by now had all gathered outside to spectate, the men stood exhausted at the edge of the cesspit.

The two mechanical predators paused momentarily as if eyeing their prey. Then with full throttle charged the men, giving them no choice but to hurl themselves into the stinking cesspit as the planes gracefully left the ground and rose into the air to the rapturous applause from the female population of the airfield. Connie and Joy flew alongside each other with a victorious thumbs up then turned towards their assigned destinations.

The small teenage girl, at the controls of an old plane, could barely see over the front of the cockpit. A much younger Joseph was sitting behind her at the duel controls offering some encouraging words.
"That's good Maggie…good…now reduce some of the power but keep her flying level. Now pull back as if you're trying to stop her from landing. Let her sink to the ground slowly. Brilliant, the best yet I think ja?"

"I felt really good about that one Joseph. I think I'm ready to do one on my own." Said the young Maggie.

"In time, in time." Laughed Joseph.

Maggie's daydream was interrupted by an unfamiliar voice.

"Excuse me, are you a nurse?"

She looked across the railway compartment as she left the pleasant reminiscing that she was so enjoying. A young army captain was smiling at her.

"What?" said Maggie.

"I can't place your uniform." Said the officer, "are you some sort of nurse?"

Maggie was a little put out by the remark but answered. "Actually I'm a midwife. I deliver babies."

"Why the wings?" the young man enquired as he pointed to the fabric wings on Maggie's tunic.

"Surely you've heard of the stork?" replied Maggie, "you know the thing with wings that delivers babies."

The officer replied somewhat apologetically. "I get the feeling I've just made a bit of a blunder and then been put in my place."

Maggie smiled back saying, "I'm sorry, I couldn't resist it. But I do deliver babies…to men. Some with single engines and some with four."

"You're a pilot, but I thought…"

"Pilots were men?" questioned Maggie. "Well don't worry about the war effort, we're not allowed to touch the guns or drop bombs. That's strictly for the boys."

The eager young officer leant forward and enquired. "That's still sounds pretty amazing. How long have you been doing this?"

"Ah that's where you catch me out," confessed Maggie. "I'm on my way to collect my first one."

"Thank heavens for that," said the officer, "it was getting a bit thirty love wasn't it? My name's John Butler."

"Maggie Stewart." Smiled Maggie.

As they both leant forward to shake hands a steward popped his head into the compartment. "Buffets open madam, sir."

"What would you say to a stewed cup of railway tea and a stale sandwich?" asked John.

"Yuk?" questioned Maggie.

John got up and slid back the compartment door "I agree but we as don't have any options and I'm parched…care to join me? Maggie smiled, "You've talked me into it. Spam and limp lettuce here we come."

They left the compartment and headed towards the buffet car along the crowded corridor of soldiers and kit bags. Inside the buffet they found it to be equally packed and were forced to stand very close together, which didn't seem to bother either of them. Eventually they managed to get a seat but John was compelled to give his up for the pregnant wife of a young corporal. The look on Maggie's face suggested approval of such a gesture.

They were at ease in each other's company swopping their histories and ambitions. John was genuinely fascinated with Maggie's story.

"Wow, I feel I've had a pretty sheltered and privileged life in comparison," he commented.

"So where did all the sheltering take place?" questioned Maggie.

"Oh various," replied John. "My father's regiment was stationed in Egypt during the early 20's which was where I first made an appearance. Then it was back to England and a very structured education of public school, Oxford and Sandhurst. Not what you would call the real world."

"Maybe not, but I can think of a few people who have had similar upbringings and think it is." Maggie smiled.

"I'll take that as a compliment," said John.

"Now about this stork you claim to resemble," John took out a pen from his pocket and drew a cartoon stork on a paper napkin.

Maggie laughed at the drawing. "That's really funny and very good. Ever thought of taking it up professionally?" said Maggie.

"Funny you should say that. It was either be a poor struggling artist or follow the family tradition and a life of kaki for king and country." Said john.

"So tradition won." Said Maggie.

"Afraid so, after a fairly long period of persuasion from one particularly worried parent."

"Dad?" Questioned Maggie.

"Correct," answered John.

Liking the sensitivity that she'd just discovered Maggie probed a little more.

"And you still draw?"

"Lots," replied John. "One day I will have that studio bathed in northern light where I can splash paint on canvasses to my hearts content."

The steward arrived to clear the table and went to take the napkin. Maggie reached for it first, folded it and put it into her tunic pocket. They carried on talking until the train reached Maggie's stop. There was an awkward moment of saying goodbye. Too early to give Maggie a peck on the cheek John shook Maggie's hand then held onto it with both hands. She pulled away nervously. John looked embarrassed as he took a step back. They parted mutually frustrated.

A few days later Maggie had just finished delivering another plane. She pulled the documents from her pocket to hand over to the receiving officer. John's drawing of the stork fell onto the table. The officer looked at it and handed it back to Maggie. She stood gazing at it for a moment and smiled.

Miles away John was inspecting a parade of soldiers. A stern looking Sergeant Major was walking by his side. As John stopped to inspect a young soldier his attention wandered as he remembered Maggie's voice.
"Surely you've heard of the stork. You know, the thing with wings that delivers babies?"

John smiled to himself. The young soldier, who thought John was smiling at him, smiled back. The Sergeant Major gave them both a suspicious look. John, realising the confusion that he had caused, snapped out of it and strode off saying.

"Very good Sergeant Major, carry on."

Meanwhile Maggie was airborne with a new delivery. She looked all around her, enjoying the freedom of the clear blue sky. She pulled the drawing a little way from her top pocket to check if it was still there and pushed it back again causing an even bigger grin to spread across her face. That smile lasted well into the evening as she arrived back at White Waltham on the bus from the railway station.

She walked slowly, exhausted and pleased by a rewarding day of doing what she loved. She passed a small florist delivery van leaving the airfield, not realising that it could have anything to do with her.

Propped up against the door of her billet was a bunch of roses. Curiously Maggie took the card attached to the flowers. That smile was emphasised again as she read.

"Congratulations on your first delivery. John X.

Chapter five
Better than sex

Joy was standing opposite Fishwick's desk. He slid a few papers across to her. Joy flicked through them disdainfully as she asked. "What's this?"

Without looking up Fishwick gave the textbook reply. "It's called a Lysander. Capable of very short field landings and flying very slow…ideal for agent work.

Unimpressed, Joy commented. "Why don't you just give me a bicycle with wings and be done with it?"

Fishwick was quick to reply as he peered over his glasses. "If the Air Ministry had such a machine nothing would give me greater pleasure. In the meantime you'll have to make do with the Lysander…now if you'll excuse me?

Joy's lips tightened in anger as she dramatically span on one heel and left an unconcerned Fishwick.

In the weeks that followed supply and demand for relocating existing aircraft and delivering new ones seemed to go into overdrive. Maggie painted a scoreboard type sign, incorporating John's drawing of the stork next to the three girls names showing what and how many aircraft each of them had delivered. Connie's camera was in constant use recording everything that she got to fly. As for poor Joy, she continued to fly all manner of slow and archaic aircraft that had been assigned to her. Maggie and John's romance had developed the best it could under the circumstances of snatching moments at railway stations and brief telephone calls. And above all, a friendship and dependency never experienced before by all three women had strengthened.

Maggie and Connie were sitting in deckchairs enjoying a rare welcome break from their somewhat hectic flying schedule on a mid summer afternoon in 1940. A bored looking Joy approached reading a magazine. From a few yards away she heard what the other two were talking about.

"How many Spitfires have you done now Con?" said Maggie.

"Lost count." Replied Connie. "In fact I'm getting rather fed up with them. I long for an old string bag so I can relax and watch the world go by."

"I know what you mean," said Maggie "these Spits are very exciting but they do take it out of you. Hi Joy." Continued Maggie, "Mackerel wants to see you – urgent delivery apparently."

"I hate you two sometimes." Snapped Joy. "I suppose you might as well put me down on the board for another airborne sewing machine…that's if you can be bothered to get off your bums."

Demonstrating another dramatic exit Joy marched off towards Fishwick's office.

"I hope you're right Mags or I'm gonna feel terrible." Said Connie.

Maggie tried her best to answer through hysterical laughter. "Trust me I've fixed everything. He's not as bad as he seems…come on."

They both got up and sheepishly followed Joy at a safe and unseen distance.

Without knocking Joy bursts into Fishwick's office and barked, "Right, let's have it, handling notes and bike clips. Fishwick casually slid the papers across to Joy in the way she had become all too familiar with. Joy grabbed the papers, started to thumb through them, and then was suddenly frozen in disbelief.

"It's a Spit…a Spitfire…a brand new one. Oh God, oh Christ, oh shit! Mumbled Joy.

"If you don't show a little more restraint wit your language young lady I'll change my mind." Said Fishwick.

Joy backed out of the door, bumping into a chair and a filing cabinet on her way.
"Sorry sir and thank you…thank you very much indeed. Thank you sir." Said Joy.

As she left the tiniest hint of a smile come across Fishwick's face. He corrected this however as he noticed Maggie and Connie peering in through the window.
"So what did you get?" asked Maggie as Joy closed the door behind her.

"As if you didn't know." Smiled Joy clutching the Spitfire papers. "How about showing me around."

"It'll be our pleasure." Said Connie.

As the threesome walked towards the spitfire Joy enthusiastically, tucked her hair into her flying helmet then stopped about fifty yards away from the lone aircraft and said,

"Oh my god, look at it."

"We've taken the liberty of packing your usual caviar sandwiches M'lady." Joked Maggie.

"Oh you darlings, you shouldn't have." Answered Joy in all seriousness.

Maggie and Connie looked at each other and smiled pathetically as another joke fell on deaf ears.

Maggie and Connie stood on a wing each and leant into the cockpit to offer the benefit of their experience to Joy who sat and stoked the control column in a world of her own, not really hearing anything at all from her two friends.

A few moments passed before Joy took to the air under the watchful eyes of Maggie and Connie.
"Nice take off." Said Connie "She's been ready for that for weeks."
"Old Fishwick certainly made her appreciate it." Answered Maggie.
Fishwick smiled to himself as he heard the roar of the Spitfire's Merlin engine overhead.

Joy was finally at the controls of a Spitfire. Her slight nervousness was somewhat obvious by the way she was talking to herself.

She gave the aeroplane a little more power and was instantly pushed back in her seat.

"More power…heavens."

Gaining more confidence Joy curiously attempted some more advanced flying maneuvers as she spoke to her new companion.

"Right my darling, before I introduce you to your new daddy let's see what you can do."

She pulled back on the control column sending the Spitfire into a steep climb before disappearing into a cloud.

"Oh my god this beats sex." She said out loud.

After a few seconds the Spitfire re-emerged from the cloud. It wasn't however alone. It was virtually alongside the Spitfire's adversary…a Messerschmitt 109. Inside the

German fighter a young pilot was nervously and desperately looking at a map and trying to get a fix on landmarks down below.

Joy suddenly noticed she had company "oh shit!" she said to herself.

The Luftwaffe rookie didn't react the way that Joy was expecting however.
Whether his guns were empty or the idea of going into battle with what he may have thought was an RAF fighter ace flying a feared Spitfire no one will ever know.
He rolled his aircraft over slid back the canopy and baled out.

Joy flew on, somewhat surprised, confused but happy to be alone again.

She landed at her destination airfield and reported in. A flight sergeant was sitting at a small desk. A young airman was standing behind him. The Sergeant looked up as joy entered and handed over the papers.

"One Spitfire all present and correct." Said Joy.

"Any faults, problems or niggles?" asked the Flight Sergeant.

"No" replied Joy, "but I did have a 109 down near Chelmsford."

Both men looked at each other before the Sergeant spoke.

"You what?

"There is one less fighter for the Luftwaffe in, what I would imagine various pieces in the Essex countryside." Replied Joy.

How could you? Your guns weren't armed."

"Didn't need them" replied Joy. "The chap just got out."

"Don't be ridiculous," argued the Flight Sergeant. "Here's your meal voucher."

He handed over a slip of paper with NAAFI printed on it.

"Suit yourself," replied Joy "but I really would suggest that you check with the local constabulary."

"And I'll decide whether to phone up and confirm a fairy story." Replied the Sergeant.

Joy shrugged her shoulders and left as the young airman leant over to his Sergeant.

"Shall I phone Chelmsford Sarg?"

"Yeah alright." Replied the Flight Sergeant reluctantly.

An RAF officer and plain-clothes police officer were standing over the young German pilot who was seated in a small interview room at Chelmsford police station sipping a mug of tea. The phone rang and the policeman picked it up and listened. "That's right, picked him up about an hour ago." Said the policeman. He listened again then spoke with a curious smile on his face. "A what?...a girl?"

Some time later Maggie and Connie were sitting outside their hut having both just returned from their daily deliveries. Maggie was reading an evening newspaper.
"It says here that a member of The Air Transport Auxiliary forced down an enemy fighter over South East England."

At that point Joy appeared. She walked up to the Storks scoreboard and instead of putting a tick next to her name she drew a swastika in true fighter pilot fashion of claiming a kill. Maggie and Connie both looked at each other in disbelief as Joy smiled sweetly, dusted off her hands and went into the hut saying, "not a bad first date."

"No..it couldn't have been. Could it?" asked Connie.
Maggie and Connie both shouted in unison as they rushed into the hut to follow Joy.
"Joy?"

Chapter six
Boys and girls come out to play

Maggie and John were sitting up in bed. They were gazing over the top of their uniform jackets on the backs of two chairs at a sea view through a small hotel window. The thought of carrying on from what they had been doing the night before was disturbed by a knock at the door.
"Who could that be?" Asked a startled Maggie.

"Breakfast I suppose." Replied John casually. "Ordered it last night. Thought we would need to build our strength up."

"They'll see us in bed." Panicked Maggie.

"You mean just like a married couple." Suggested John.

"It's obvious we're not…I'm not here," said Maggie as she disappeared under the bed covers.

"Come in please," shouted John

A young waitress entered carrying a tray that she placed onto a table.

"Would you like me to set it out sir?" she asked.

John lifted up a corner of the covers and asked Maggie. "Would you like her to set it out?"

A distant muffled sound came from under the covers. "No"

The waitress left, biting her lip trying not to laugh.

"You can come out now." Said John

"Pig" said Maggie looking all hot and sweaty.

"Well one things for sure," said John, "you don't do this sort of thing very often."

"I suppose you do then?" questioned Maggie.

"You're the first." Replied John

"`Really?" asked Maggie

"Well the first pilot that is" said John.

"You smooth bastard." Said Maggie narrowing her eyes.

"Steady on, there is one significant difference." John continued.

"What I scored a nine?" asked Maggie sarcastically

"No, I love you." Said John. "And actually you score a nine and a half."

By now Maggie was out of bed and heading for the breakfast tray. She had her back to John not showing him how pleased she was with his remark. While John enjoyed looking at her naked body Maggie announced.

"I was thinking of showing you off next week..."

John tried to interrupt

"Er"

"Just a small local pub. Connie and her brother Bob will be there and…" she tried to continue but was interrupted again.

"Maggie?" pleaded John

"And Joy and her boyfriend Jimmy…"

"Maggie, come and sit down." Said John

Maggie sat down on the corner of the bed as John put a robe around her shoulders and held her tightly.

"Sorry, I didn't mean to push you." Said Maggie

John starts to explain. "It's not…"

Maggie attempted to carry on.

"If you don't want to get involved I…"

John put his finger tenderly to Maggie's lips.

"Maggie, shut up. You're not pushing me and it's nothing to do with getting involved. You know that half the regiment is in the Far East?

"Yes," replied Maggie.

"Well, as from next week, so will the other half." Continued John

"I see," said Maggie with a look of relief and obvious concern.

"Now listen," said John, "a minute ago I told you something that I've never told anyone before. Have you got something to tell me?"

Maggie looked up into John's eyes then looked away as she said, "No, everything that I've ever loved has either died or gone away, so I'll never tell you I love you."

John moved into Maggie's eye-line and asked softly. "Can I take that as a yes then?"

"Yes," said Maggie. "When do you go?"

"Day after tomorrow." Replied John.

"Right, better get back down to it then." Said Maggie throwing off the robe and sliding back into bed. Both were conscious of a desire to make up for what they were going to miss during the unknown future as they exhausted each other with erotic pleasure and an intense feeling of love.

Eventually they lay stoking each other, trickles of sweat shared their bodies.

John turned towards Maggie. "Looks like breakfast has gone cold. Shall I order some more?"

"No," said Maggie "Let's have lunch at that little café on the pier."

"Lunch isn't for a couple of hours yet." Said John kissing Maggie's breast.

"What could we possibly do for a couple of hours?" asked Maggie rolling over on top of John.

"Work up an appetite?" said John sliding his hands down Maggie's thighs.

"Correct." Whispered Maggie.

An intense week of flying, for all three women, passed quickly. The evening air was still warm as Romak got out of his 1939 red MG and looked up at The Hop Poles sign swinging gently in the summer breeze. He went in and looked around for a friendly face.

"Hey Pole, anyone for cricket?" said Bob stepping from behind a large country gentleman at the bar.

Bob smiled and tugged the tunic of Bob's uniform.

"You haven't changed much then scruff." Replied Romak.

"Don't you know anything?" answered Bob. "It's tradition for a fighter pilot to leave the top button of his tunic undone."

"And I suppose it comes in handy that girls recognise who the brave and fearless knights of the air are hey?" replied Romak with a smile.

"I wouldn't know about that" said Bob "I'm just not prepared to argue with tradition."

"Lying shit." Said Romak.

"Come and meet the others said Bob."
Bob put his hand on Romak's shoulder and guided him towards a corner of the lounge bar of the pub where Maggie, Connie, Joy and Jimmy were seated around a small table.

"So what made you choose the Navy Jimmy?" asked Connie.
"Joy took me flying and I thought I would rather drown than do that again." Replied Jimmy.
"That's a bit harsh." Commented Joy.
"So was that flight," said Jimmy. "I much prefer the thought of being torpedoed."
Bob and Romak arrived at the table.
Bob wasted no time in making an announcement.
"OK everyone, this is my friend Romak and as he has more than once told me himself,

Poland's finest cricketer. Romak, this is Maggie, Joy and Jimmy. Connie you already know."

"Only sort of know," said Connie. "About thirty seconds in the university bar."

"I didn't know you were so quick Romak, you old rouge." Teased Bob.

Connie turned to Bob with a narrowed eyed look.

"Is that all you can think of? Romak knows what I mean."

"Of course I do Connie," smiled Romak "Now what I would really like to know is the other side to this brother of yours. I've only ever heard his story and it's all a bit too glowing to be true. What I need is some real good blackmail material – the sort of stuff that his squadron over there would love to hear."

Romak pointed to the other side of the bar where a group of pilots were having a drink. Connie smiled at the thought of the opportunity. "Sit down" she said. "This could be a long night."

"I don't think I want to hear this," said Bob
"Come on Jimmy, half a crown says The Royal Air Force can kick the arse of The Royal Navy at darts."
"Sound like an easy half crown, 'scuse us girls." Said Jimmy.
Romak and Connie sat down at a small table as Bob and Jimmy made their way to the darts board. Maggie and Joy were left together. After a moments silence between them, Maggie looked up from her drink and asked Joy.

"Do you think, one day, you'll ever get married?"

"What Jimmy you mean?" answered Joy "No he's a sweetheart and I'm terribly fond of him but not in a settling down sort of way."

"Not necessarily Jimmy." continued Maggie. "I mean, anybody."

"If it means giving up flying then no." said Joy.

Maggie continued. "But how can you say that? How do you know that someone won't just come along and change everything for that, near as damn it, perfect life?"

"Maggie, I've had that near as damn it perfect life for most of my life and it's very bloody boring. For the first time I've found something that's difficult and exciting and no one is going to do it for me and I'm going to stick to it like glue. Maybe someone will come along but he'll have a tough act to follow." Answered Joy very determinedly. "Any way, it's a jolly strange question for you to be asking. You haven't met someone likely to clip your wings have you?"

"I don't know," replied Maggie sheepishly "No of course not, don't be silly."

"I think we're both too much in love with the smell of aeroplane fuel to suddenly find the small of baby bum talcum powder attractive." Said Joy. "If you want to see the marrying kind, look over there." Joy gestured towards Connie who was getting on extremely well with Romak.

The laughter from Connie and Romak's table confirmed Joy's observation.

"Mom said when he was six he'd blown all his pocket money so hc put on one of her dresses and tried to convince me he was the tooth fairy and had come to take the money back." Said Connie.

"Fantastic, did she take any photos?" Asked Romak

"Afraid not" answered Connie.

"What a shame" said Romak, "that would have been perfect for the squadron notice board."

"So what about you. Can you say what you do at the War Office?' questioned Connie

"Let's just say I work toward the downfall of the Nazis," said Romak

"That could mean anything from secret agent to head of paper clips" said a frustrated Connie"

"One day I'll tell you" smiled Romak

Connie seemed to like the idea that there was going to be a "one day" as she answered, "I'll hold you to that"

The look into each other's eyes was disturbed by Bob and the others appearing at their table as the landlord rang the time bell.
"Come on you two bye-byes time." Teased Bob
"It might be a bit of a squeeze but Earnest should be able to fit us all in." said Joy
"You didn't drag poor old Earnest all this way did you?" said Connie
"'Course" said Joy "he loves it and I did take a ginger beer out to him about an hour ago"
"Bet he loved that" whispered Maggie to Connie.
"I could take one in my car if you want to come with me Connie?" asked Romak

"Connie smiled as Romak helped her on with her coat.
Joy commented to Maggie as the couple walked past them.
"Do you smell talcum powder?"
"You know, I think I do" Answered Maggie.

Apart from Connie and Romak who seemed to be in perfect control, the rest of them somewhat staggered out of the pub to be greeted by Earnest holding open the door to the Rolls Royce whilst muttering, "All aboard for the piss artist's special"
Maggie and Joy got in first followed by Bob and Jimmy who virtually fell in.
Earnest carried on muttering, "If that's the Air Force and the Navy thank got we've got an Army.

Joy barked an order at Earnest. "First stop the station to drop the boys off then the airfield Earnest.
"Bloody 'ell" said Earnest.

About half an hour later Romak's car pulled up outside the airfield hut.

"You know I'm not sure if your brother will approve of this but I'm going to do it anyway" said Romak as he gave Connie a kiss on the cheek.
"I don't think he'll mind and Dad would certainly approve," said Connie.
"How do you know?" said Romak
"Think about it," answered Connie" I've come all this way to England and just met a very nice Polish boy"

"And I would like to see Mr. Kletzki's daughter again please" replied Romak.
"You have his permission," said Connie.
The Rolls Royce came into view as distant singing was heard from Maggie and Joy.
"Time to go" said Romak "Three against one is unfair, especially you three."
He got into his car, drove off and waved to Maggie and Joy as he passed them.

Chapter seven
Tragedy and poetry

The next few weeks gained lots of new editions to the Storks scoreboard expressing busy times and successful deliveries for all three women.

A new season had begun to make an appearance as autumn leaves decorated the corrugated roof of hut number twenty-seven.

Maggie was just leaving as Joy approached carrying her flying helmet.

"You look done in," said Maggie, a little concerned.

"Overworked and underpaid but completely fulfilled" answered Joy.

"Just take it easy," said Maggie. "It can get dangerous falling asleep at 7,000 feet.

"According to the old scoreboard you're not exactly slacking yourself," answered Joy.

"I'm more used to it." Replied Maggie

"Do as I say not as I do eh?" joked Joy.

Maggie took Joy's arm and led her back in the direction she came.

"Come on, I've got a few minutes before I'm due to take off, I'll buy you a cup of NAFFI tea."

"I've had better offers but you're on," said Joy.

They sat down at a table next to the two mechanics from the Tiger Moths incident. The men glared, got up and left the moment they recognised Joy.

"Funny old thing pride isn't it." Commented Joy

"Wonder how Connie is getting on with her first multi-engine." Said Maggie.

"All those knobs to play with." said Joy "It must be awesome flying those heavy bombers.

Meanwhile on a windy East Anglia airfield Connie was walking towards a Lancaster. Bomber. She stopped in front of it and slowly looked up. She felt like a mouse looking up at an eagle.

She said to herself, "honey you've hit the big time."

"Morning miss," a voice interrupted, "you miss Kletzi?"

It was a sprightly, weasel featured little man in his late forties.

"That's right," answered Connie.

"I'm your flight engineer, Ward's the name.

"What's your first name Mr Ward?" asked Connie

"Richard miss, Dickie if you like."

"Well Dickie, I'm Connie, shall we see if we can get this building to fly?"

He smiled and replied, "You work the throttles and I'll work the steam Miss, er Connie."

"Just one thing before we go," said Connie. She took her camera out of her bag and stepped back from the huge bomber.

"I'll have to walk to the next airfield to get this baby in."

As she lined up the Lancaster in her camera she noticed that Ward was posing next to the aeroplane as if thinking she wanted to take his picture. Connie gestured to him to move to the side. Which only caused him to take one step to the left and pose even more. "Oh what the heck." She said to herself as she took the picture resigned to the fact that she was going to capture more than just the plane on this occasion.

One by one the giant propellers burst into life, introduced by a puff of grey smoke.
"Apparently this is going to a new crew so there may well be a bit of a welcoming

committee. They get a bit keen on their first one." Said Ward

"In that case," answered Connie, "I feel a bit of a low pass might be called for so they can get a good look at it."

Ward gave out a very infectious laugh, a bit like the sound of a machine gun with the trigger stuck on fire. Connie smiled to herself as she pushed the throttle levers forward. After what seemed like forever compared with the lighter aircraft she had been flying Connie gently pulled back the control stick to lift the giant bird off the ground.

"Oh yes, come on my darling," shouted Connie.

"Beg your pardon? Oh you're talking to the Lanc thought you were talking to me Miss." Said Dickie as he gave out another burst of machine gun laughter.

"Excuse me Dickie," answered Connie, "got a bit over excited there. And it's Connie not Miss remember?"

"Sorry Miss…I mean Connie."

At a Lincolnshire airfield the eager new crew were in the briefing room waiting like expectant fathers.

The young pilot spoke up. "Listen I can hear it – come on you lot."

They all grabbed bikes outside and headed off across the airfield. Connie was on her final approach for landing. She looked down to see the strange looking bicycle convoy snaking its way across the grass.

"Must be the proud new Daddies," said Connie, "let's give them that closer look.

Ward fired off a few more rounds of his distinctive laugh.

On the ground the crew saw the bomber turn towards them.

"Christ it's veered off the runway." Shouted the pilot.

"It's coming straight at us," panicked another of the crew.

The huge bomber flew overhead with a thunderous roar causing the crew to crash into each other with their bikes leaving a tangled mass of spokes, handlebars and bodies.

Connie banked the Lancaster over and made a second approach to landing, which to Ward's admiration was perfect. "Nicely done Connie."

The young pilot however wasn't so impressed. He stomped over to the bomber as Connie was just dropping down from the pilot's hatch onto the ground with her back to the angry airman.

"What the fuck do you think you're doing with my aeroplane, you dozy bastard?" he shouted.
"Language young man, ladies on board," said Ward joining Connie.
"Yours is it," said Connie, "my God you barely look old enough. Well I suppose the RAF know what they're doing. Don't forget now check the tyre pressures regularly and no overtaking for the first one thousand miles. Realising that Connie wasn't one of the boys the whole crew was left open mouthed as Connie and Ward made their way across the airfield to the sound of Ward's laughter.

A few days later Connie and Joy were sitting outside their hut on an unusually warm autumn early afternoon. Connie was reading a letter that she had just got from Bob.

"Dear Con, sorry I haven't written sooner but things have been getting pretty busy up here lately. Gone are the days when we used to pop up and knock out the odd stray bomber. Sometimes there are hundreds of them. We've been joining forces, meeting other squadrons from other fields and putting up the most amazing attack formations. Some of the guys they're sending to us are no more than school kids with only 10 hours experience. Last week we scrambled five times in one day. We looked like shit that night. The next day we were up again first thing. Seems crazy that we all longed for action when now all we want to do is sleep."

Joy glanced up and looked past Connie to see a staff car pull up in the distance. An officer got out and went into Fishwick's office. After a few seconds he came back out this time with Fishwick. Connie continued to read, unaware of the two men approaching.

"How about this for some good news – I've been recommended for the Distinguished Flying Cross, a dead cert for impressing any girl with that bit of ribbon on my chest. How's old Romak? Yes I know what you're up to. Good choice sis he's one of the best. Can't wait till we all meet up again, that was a great evening."

Fishwick and the stranger had now arrived on the scene. He interrupted the moment

speaking in a much softer voice than both women were used to. "Connie this is squadron leader Marsden, he'd like a word with you."
Joy got up to go, "See you later Con."
Fishwick stared into Joy's eyes intently. "I think you should stay…please"
"I'm afraid I've got some very bad news for you Miss Kletzi…it's your brother Bob.

Joy stood behind Connie and held onto the doorframe of the hut to steady herself and closed her eyes waiting for the horror that she knew was sure to come. Fishwick shuffled nervously as Connie looked blankly up at Marsden.

"I'm afraid he's been killed in action."

Joy rested both hands on Connie's shoulders as silence hit the small group like a profound deafness.

"Oh God" whispered Joy. Connie's eyes widened as she stared aggressively back at Marsden. "He can't be I've got a letter from him…look."

Fishwick picked up the envelope. For the first time he called her by her first name. "Connie this was posted two days ago. Bob died this morning."

"No…you've got it wrong, it's not Bob he's a really good pilot." Connie shouted.

"Connie, Connie," pleaded Joy.

Connie rose to her feet and started to walk around. "Alright he's been shot down but he would have baled out, so he will be OK, you don't really know."

"I'm afraid we do," said Marsden, "there was an explosion and I'm sorry…no parachute." Connie's anger increased "But he's just been talking to me…look."

She grasped Bob's letter and thrust it into Marsden's face, holding it so tight that a trickle of blood ran down her wrist caused by her own finger nail embedding into the palm of her hand."

Joy reached for Connie's hand and held it affectionately.

Connie turned her back on Marsden and Fishwick saying, "please go away."

As the two men walked away, unable to do any more, Connie sat back down and after a moments silence looked up at Joy saying, in a pathetic laugh, "I don't believe them you know…it's not true."

Joy could only hold Connie tightly and say to herself, "For God's sake hurry up Maggie." The next forty minutes seemed like hours to Joy. Connie still refused to try and make any sort of sense or come to terms with the news.

Maggie walked slowly across the airfield happily swinging her flying helmet in her hand as she thought about John. In the distance she could see the tiny figures of Joy and Connie. She squinted to get a clearer view as she started to realise that Joy was holding Connie's hands. She knew something was wrong. Her pace quickened and then broke into a run. She slowed her pace a few yards away from the couple and approached nervously. Joy looked up at Maggie, her eyes full of tears. Connie just continued to stare straight at the ground showing a vacancy of all emotion.

"It's Bob Mags." Said Joy,
"Oh God." said Maggie not needing Joy to complete the tragic news.
Maggie put both hands around Connie's face and whispered, "Connie…sweetheart"
Connie lifted her tearless eyes to Maggie. Her lips parted to speak but nothing came out.
"What are we going to do?" whispered Joy
"Just be here. It's all we can do." Answered Maggie.

As the light started to fade Joy gently led Connie into the hut. Maggie wrapped her jacket around Connie's shoulders. Despite it being a warm evening it was the only thing that she could think of doing.

All three sat in silence on Connie's bed until the sound of a car screeching to a halt was heard outside. Fishwick had telephoned Romak at the War Office.

Romak appeared at the door. Connie looked up at him.

"Romak I'm having this really bad dream, can you wake me up please?"

Maggie got up from the bed leaving a space for Romak to sit beside Connie.

Romak held Connie saying, "He's gone Connie, you've got to let him go."

With a sudden determination in her voice Connie answered, "not yet, not yet."

Maggie stroked Connie's hair and Joy gave her a kiss on the forehead, as they both knew it best to leave the couple alone.

After just less than half an hour Romak reached for a piece of paper from the small table next to Connie's bed. He started to read.

"Up with me! up with me into the clouds!
For thy song, Lark, is strong;
Up with me, up with me into the clouds!
Singing, singing,
With clouds and sky about thee ringing,
Lift me, guide me till I find
That spot which seems so to thy mind!"

Connie's sudden uncontrollable crying caused Maggie and Joy to burst into the room.

All three slung their arms around Connie in a bizarre sense of relief.
"Go on my darling, as loud as you like," shouted Joy as she joined in with the crying.

Being able to start living again took a lot longer for Connie. Fishwick suspended her from flying in the interest of her own safety. Maggie and Joy spent as much time with her as they possibly could. Trying not to leave her on her own for too long. They would play cards, go for walks and think of favours and chores for her to do for them while they were away, just to keep her occupied. Even Fishwick turned up one day with a pot of paint and suggested, "As you're still getting paid, how about sprucing the place up a bit?" Connie couldn't bring herself to do it however and Fishwick didn't pursue it, as it was just his way of trying to help.

Despite Romak's efforts to bring her back from despair she existed in a world unwelcome to anyone other than herself and her departed brother. A meal in a local restaurant would result in Connie catching sight of a young pilot, causing her to sink deeper into her depression. A trip to the cinema to see Connie's favourite Marx Brothers even failed to do the trick. Weeks passed into months as Connie showed no signs of coming to terms with Bob's death. In an attempt to try anything and everything Romak took Connie to the theatre to see a comedy. The theatre was filled with laughter but Connie sat and gazed as if watching a serious play. As the comedy drew to a close

Connie felt a tap on her shoulder. She turned towards Romak to see him wearing his gas mask trying to drink through a straw. He shrugged his shoulders pathetically in a silent clown like gesture.

Connie laughed. Romak took off the mask and smiled at Connie. As everyone stood for the national anthem they both just sat and looked at each other and continued to look and smile as the theatre slowly emptied.

"Thank you." Said Connie.

A few days later Romak and Connie were driving down a country lane.

"So where are we going?" said Connie.

"That depends on you." Replied Romak cryptically.

"Meaning?" Questioned Connie as she gave a slightly puzzled look.

Romak stopped the car by the side of the road and pointed to a sign reading Cambridge.

"Think you can handle it?" asked Romak as he clasped Connie's hand.

Connie placed her other hand on top of Romak's. "Only if you can handle a few more tears," she said.

"Used to those," Romak replied as he glanced in the mirror and turned the car towards the sign. "You're doing brilliantly Con." He added.

They ambled slowly across the familiar playing field of the university grounds where so many memories filled Connie's head. Romak felt Connie's hand tighten on his every time he knew the past was both tormenting and comforting her.

Every sound seemed to be amplified to Connie: distant laughter, birds singing, and music from an open window. Her face was expressionless as her eyes and ears adjusted to the next incoming memory.

Romak looked at her without her noticing. He so desperately wanted to say something to ease her pain but couldn't think of what to say, scared that anything might cause Connie's complete collapse and thinking that he may have done the wrong thing bringing her back too soon.

She suddenly stopped walking and looked around. Romak looked at her, not knowing what to expect. He put his arm around her and waited for the worse.

Connie burst out laughing. "There are hardly any men around." She said.

This wasn't quite what Romak was expecting. "Bob would have loved it," she continued. "It's his idea of heaven, all these great looking girls and no competition. "Don't you see?"

Romak felt justified in joining in with the laughter. He felt Connie's hand relax slightly in his. It was a sensation that made him feel closer to her than he'd ever felt.

They both stopped laughing at exactly the same second. Romak held Connie's face in his hands and kissed her tenderly. Connie turned the tenderness into passion as she opened her mouth wider. Romak responded and pulled her tighter toward him.

They were completely oblivious to the more conservative locals passing by giving them disapproving looks.

Chapter eight

A girl called Amy and a bad weather day

Joy slid back the canopy hood after landing her third Hurricane fighter.

She climbed out of the tiny cockpit, gathered up her papers and headed off on a brisk walk towards the hut. Stopping outside she pulled out a pen and put another mark on the, now quite full, stork scoreboard.

"That looks rather interesting." Said a voice from behind her.

Joy turned to see a woman, a little older than her, also wearing an ATA uniform.

"Oh it's just a bit of fun really…and to convince us how hard we're working" said Joy. "Have you just joined?" she continued.

"No I'm just passing through." Said the newcomer. "I'm based at Hatfield…collecting some spares for Biggin Hill.

"Well I'm Joy, pleased to meet you."

"Amy," said the woman. "Sorry should have introduced myself earlier."

"What are you flying?" Asked Joy

"A Harvard." Answered Amy.

"You want to watch out for those things," said Joy, "can swing terribly on take-off."

"Really? I'll remember that." Said Amy.

"I'm just going to make some tea if you're interested." Said Joy

Amy smiled. "I'll give you a hand."

As they sat down outside in a couple of battered armchairs with their RAF issue mugs, Joy continued the questioning.

"Flown any Spits?" She asked.

"A few yes," answered Amy. "Just a minute you're not the Joy… Joy Bamford who forced down the 109 are you?"

"Well yes," answered Joy a little coyly, "but don't believe all you read. There wasn't a lot of forcing to do. He looked about twelve and if he had seen who was at the controls of the Spitfire I don't think I would be here now."

"All the same, it's a hell of a story for the grandchildren." Said Amy.

The afternoon wore on through various mugs of tea as they continued to chat like old friends. Joy taking the lead in the conversation as Joy always did.

"Have you done many flights?" asked Joy.

"Sort of lost count," said Amy.

"Wait till you get into the long distance stuff, that can be pretty tiring." Joy informed Amy.

"Really?" answered Amy somewhat innocently.

"They tend to familiarise you with as many types as possible at first and when you think you can cope with anything they drop a long distance on you…how's your navigation skills?"

"Oh not bad…haven't got lost yet." Replied Amy

Joy leaped straight in with a comment "Well you probably will when you start going further afield it can be quite an experience. Oh don't I sound gloomy…must be terrifying you?"

"Not at all, don't worry, I'm a big girl." Laughed Amy.

Joy continued the questioning. "So what aeronautical adventures have you had?"

"Well nothing compared with your little dogfight." Answered Amy.

"Hardly a dogfight," said Joy, "more like a frightened rabbit."

They both laughed and enjoyed each other's company for a few more sips of tea before Amy brought the enjoyable afternoon to an end.

"Well if I don't get these spares delivered soon they'll be obsolete before they get there."

As Amy got up to leave she put her hand on Joys shoulder. "Drop in to see me when you're passing Joy. Thanks for the tea and the chat."

Felling pretty pleased with herself Joy gave a final wave to Amy as she walked across the airfield to her waiting areoplane. Joy saw Amy pass Fishwick. Fishwick acknowledged Amy as he approached Joy still sipping her tea.

"Hope you learned something" said Fishwick.
"What do you mean?" asked Joy.
Fishwick continued, "You know who that was?" asked Fishwick.
"A nice girl called Amy?" asked Joy a little sarcastically.
"Amy Johnson to be exact." Said Fishwick as he continued to walk towards his office.
"Oh shit!" said Joy as she put her hand over her eyes, separating her fingers only

slightly to see Amy's plane dipping its wing as it flew overhead.
Fishwick gave a rare chuckle on hearing Joy's embarrassed reaction.

The next day brought rain, lots of it. Through a thunderous sky it was bouncing off the wings of parked aircraft. A young ground crew airman, holding his coat over his head ran towards the mess hall, he burst in and headed for Maggie and Joy playing cards at a small table. Joy was in the process of telling Maggie her brief encounter with her new-found famous aviator friend.

"So there I was telling Amy Johnson how to fly a Harvard." Said Joy. "It was so embarrassing."

"I'm sure you're imagining it to be worse than it was." Said Maggie trying to make light of it and control the laughter at the same time.
Joy continued. "But then I gave her the benefit of my knowledge by asking her if she'd ever done any long-distance flying."
"Oh dear." Said Maggie in a high pitch voice.
"It was about as subtle as challenging Douglas Bader to a sprint to the NAFFI."
Maggie finally cracked up in front of a somewhat bemused Joy who very soon joined in with the laughter herself.

They looked up to see the young airman standing over them dripping wet.
"How many times have I told you not to take a bath with your clothes on?" asked Maggie.
"Fishwick wants to see you two now," said the, unamused young, man.

"Oh God what does Mackerel want?" asked Joy "Surely he's not intending to send us up in this?"

"He's in the radio room talking to one of your lot. Sounds like she's in a bit of trouble." Said the young man.

"Connie!" shouted Maggie.

With no time or thought to grab coats or umbrellas Maggie and Joy ran out of the mess hall and headed for the radio room. Neither of them seemed to care or notice how wet they were when they arrived to hear the radio operator telling Fishwick:

"She's saying she's going to descend and take a look...I've seen it before. They start to trust their own instincts rather than their instruments...it's very dangerous, she's getting to the stage when she'll believe what she wants to believe… she's very tired and is starting to get disorientated."

Maggie and Joy could only stare at Fishwick waiting for an explanation.
"It's Connie Kletzi – you'd better talk to her while it's still possible." Said Fishwick.
Maggie quickly sat down at the radio as the radio operator handed her the microphone. She desperately tried to compose herself before attempting to come across less concerned than she obviously was.
"Con it's Mags…how come you're up there when even the birds are walking?"
Connie's distorted voice echoed round the tiny radio room. "Maggie, at last a sensible voice. Has that jerk gone for his tea break at last?"

Maggie gave a slightly embarrassed grin to the radio operator. Joy just stared manically at the radio.

"Sorry about this Mags," said Connie, "It'll teach me not to leave without an umbrella."

"Or to check the forecast," muttered Fishwick.

"Don't worry Con you'll be OK." Said Maggie as she looked at Joy not really believing what she'd just said.

"If only I could drop down for a quick look at the situation and see a place to land." Said Connie.

Maggie didn't hesitate on coming straight back with some very firm views on Connie's comment. "Just stay with it and keep your height, fly by instruments, don't trust your head, remember the training. You could be upside down in less than two minutes and not realise it."

"I know you're right Mags, but I'm just so damn tired." Answered Connie, her voice starting to get a little faint. "And I've got a terrible guts ache…if you know what I mean?"
"You mean your monthly," asked Maggie.
"Yes and a right humdinger." Answered Connie.
Fishwick took an embarrassed step backwards, unfamiliar with such information from a pilot.

Maggie turned to Fishwick her face pleading for help. Fishwick moved Maggie's hand off the transmit button and spoke to the radio operator.

"Ring around everywhere within fifty miles, find a break in the clouds, a window or any let up in this weather. It's the only chance she's got. Joy's eyes widened at the horror of what Fiskwick had just said.

Maggie pressed a trembling finger onto the transmit button again.
"Con we're just checking the best place to get you down. You know what I mean, whoever has the most comfy beds, the best canteen and a pub within walking distance."

"I'd settle for a ploughed field as long as I could see both ends of it." Replied Connie.
"That's the spirit but I'm sure we can do better than that," relied Maggie as she noticed Joy wiping some of the condensation from the

window. In the far distance of the airfield she noticed two airmen tying down an aircraft, as the rain and wind got worse. Fishwick also looked out as he fumbled with his pipe.

As Maggie continued to comfort and support Connie, Joy frantically wrote down telephone numbers from the airfield operations directory and handed them to the radio operator. After what seemed like a lifetime the tension was broken.

"Bingo!" shouted the radio operator as he slammed down the phone and handed Maggie a piece of paper. "Got one."

Maggie took the scrap of paper and stared at it in disbelief for a second.

She showed it to Joy. "Oh my god," whispered Joy.

Maggie turned to the microphone and leant in closely.

"Con this is going to take a bit of believing but there's about half an hours cloud base lift over North Weald."

Maggie waited for the response that she was expecting.

"Bob's old station?" replied Connie.

"Yes," said Maggie, "and you've got to get there now. Think of it as an omen, fate or big brother to the rescue but just get there. Do you need a course to fly?"

"Yes please," said Connie, "and a bottle of Bob's favourite bourbon."

"OK steer one five zero," said Maggie, "When you're about ten miles out descend to five hundred feet. There are no obstructions even if you're a bit off course and you'll have a fairly good visual of the field but remember get your approach spot on, you won't have time for two attempts."

"No pressure then?" said Connie. "You'll stay with me won't you?"

"Of course," answered Maggie, "just concentrate on what you're doing we'll still be here."

Joy leaned into the microphone to offer a few words of encouragement. "Go on Con show the RAF you can fly the arse off any of them."

Even under such tense circumstances Fishwick still managed to raise a disapproving eyebrow.

A collection of emergency vehicle's, engines ticking over, were poised on either side of North Weald airfield. Sat in one of them were a middle-aged ambulance man and a young woman. They stared up into the sky through the drizzle and murk of the late afternoon that looked more like midnight.

In the far distance a tiny speck appeared, tossed around by an aggressive cross wind as if playing its final card in a game of survival.

The rain started to beat down heavier on the roof of the ambulance.

"There she is," said the ambulance man. "Come on Miss don't make us work for a living."

Back in the radio room Maggie and Joy were huddled round the radio holding hands.

Maggie took the, now tattered looking, drawing of the stork that John had given her from her top pocket. She put it to her lips and held it there.

The silence in the room seemed to amplify the rain hitting the window.

Joy leant forward to turn up the volume on the radio receiver but discovered that it was already on full volume.

"Just checking," said Joy

The radio operator gave a sympathetic smile. Suddenly there was a slight crackle from the speaker signifying that the transmit button had been pressed.

"I'm down," came the distant sounding voice, "will you come and tuck me in now please Maggie?"

Over Joy's hysterical shrieking Maggie answered, "You sod off Kletzi I need a drink."

Maggie slipped the drawing back into her pocket, sat back and gave a deep sigh.

Fishwick tapped the top of a filing cabinet in time with his words before regaining his normal composure.

"Good, good, splendid…right ladies, let that be a lesson to you. Always get an accurate forecast, never go by your instincts, trust your instruments…"

He was still lecturing as Maggie and Joy slipped out of the room.

Connie taxied her plane towards a row of Nissan huts followed by the emergency vehicles. She parked, slid back the canopy and climbed out. As soon as she touched the ground she collapsed with exhaustion into the arms of the ambulance driver.

He held her for a few seconds, shielding her face from the rain with his hand.

Connie soon came round looking up into the smiling man's eyes.

"Gee sorry about," that she said.

"Don't worry miss it's not very often that a pilot makes an old man very happy."

That typical summer afternoon weather was followed by another typical summer morning but this time in complete contrast – a clear blue sky with not even a hint of a breeze. Connie emerged from the Nissan hut kitted out and ready to continue her journey. As she approached the small waiting aeroplane she stopped in her tracks. A sudden attack of nervousness had sneaked up on her, recalling the tension of the previous day.

"Nice day for flying Miss," came a voice from behind her.

Connie turned to see the ambulance man leaning on the side of his truck with a bacon sandwich in one hand and a mug of tea in the other.

Connie smiled at him regained her confidence and carried on walking. She aimed her box camera at the plane before walking round it to do the usual checks then climbed into the cockpit.

Pushing the throttle forward she accelerated down the runway.
The ambulance man put his tea down on the fender of the ambulance and crossed his fingers. The aeroplane left the ground for a perfect take off.
The man slowly uncrossed his fingers and picked up his mug and whispered: "look after yourself girl."

Chapter nine
Bitter pills of war

Maggie glanced up to see the skylark singing high above her as she walked around the Spitfire checking if everything was how it should be. A young airman, refueling the plane called out to her. "Soon be ready ma'am."

"Don't rush," said Maggie, "It's so nice to be outside and I'm in good company."

She smiled as she raised her eyes towards the skylark. The young man looked up and smiled too.

"Nice day for a bit of flying." said the young man. "Going far?"

"Just popping over to Duxford," said Maggie. "Delivering this little baby to her new proud father."

"Let's hope they have a long and happy life together." Continued the airman.

The gatehouse guard appeared on the scene and called out to Maggie.

"Miss Stewart?"

"Yes," said Maggie.

"There's a gentleman to see you Miss. He's in the guardroom waiting…only I couldn't let him through as he doesn't have a pass…a Mr. Butler."

Maggie threw her bags down by the Spitfire's wheel and rushed off at full sprint towards the guardroom.

She called back to the young airman. "Won't be long, just got to give the Army a bollocking."

"All go isn't it?" Laughed the young man.

With the hugest grin on her face she burst into the guardroom, shouting as she threw back the door.

"One sodding letter in two months, you call that love?"

A tall distinguished looking man in his sixties stepped from the shadow of the corner of the guardhouse.

Maggie stood rigid to the spot, taken completely by surprise. "I'm sorry, I was told…I mean…I thought you were…"

"God, how stupid of me," said the man "I should have realised…I wasn't thinking. Maggie I'm Paul, John's father"

Maggie turned her head to look away from Paul Butler. She gazed out of the guardroom window looking angry at the prospect of bad news tracking her down and tormenting her like it had so many times before.

Mr. Butler continued slowly and sensitively. "I'm afraid… Look wouldn't you like to sit down?"

Maggie just shook her head without saying a word.

He continued with tears in his eyes that looked like they had been there for a long time.

"John, my son, your John has been killed"

"How?" asked Maggie in an almost robotic tone.

"Landmine, him and three others,"

"Are they sure it was him?" Questioned Maggie desperately.

"Yes," answered Paul "Oh yes…Fiona my wife…John's mother wanted to come, we've both heard a lot about you through John, but she couldn't. She's not up to much at the moment, blames me a bit really…same regiment you see…always been proud of him for that I have.

"When?" Asked Maggie.

"He joined about two years ago, straight from…"

"When did he die?" asked Maggie

"Sorry," said Mr. Butler realising his mistake. "Two days ago."

Maggie continued on the emotionless tact that was protecting her from the devastation that was really filling her heart.

"Thank you for telling me so quickly, we weren't engaged or anything you know."

Paul reached for Maggie's hand but withdrew at the last second. It reminded Maggie of John's similar gesture of affection when they first met on the train.

"He was going to bring you home, told us so. Fiona asked me to tell you you're always welcome. To come and stay that is."

The battle that Maggie was fighting with her emotions was becoming unbearable. Everything that Paul Butler said gave her a searing pain in her chest. The dryness in her mouth was choking her.

"No…no. sorry…but don't worry about your wife, she just needs to blame someone at the moment." Said Maggie.

Mr. Butler smiled as best he could. "You're just like he said, tough nut he called you. Meant it with bags of affection though.
Maggie stepped backward towards the door. "I'm going to have to go now and do my little bit for the war. Thank you for coming."
The moment she turned away to open the door tears filled her eyes. She fumbled with the door handle like a frustrated prisoner trying to flee their cell.
"There's just one thing," Mr. Butler called out. "Er, there's the funeral."

She tugged at the door, finally freeing the catch. She didn't look back when she said: "I can't…no…I just can't…sorry"

Whipping her eyes on her tunic sleeve as she ran, she could only think of one thing. Getting up into the sky where she could release her pain in privacy. Where she could scream, shout and cry without being seen by anyone.

Connie's plane had just landed. She got out and saw Maggie running towards her aircraft. Shielding her eyes from the sun she jumped down from the wing and called out.
"Maggie!"
She started to run after her, nearly knocking over a couple of ground crew airmen in the process. "Mags."

Stumbling along in her awkward flying boots she stopped to pull them off and continued to sprint in bare feet to try and catch her friend. She had so much to tell and thank Maggie for after her bad weather flight.

She threw her heavy flying jacket to the ground in a last attempt to reach her.

"Maggie wait…Maggie!"

Maggie's Spitfire took off leaving Connie still running. She stopped and stamped her foot.

"Shit!"

Fishwick appeared on the scene wondering what all the shouting was about.

Connie turned towards him and asked a question that was impossible to answer.

"She must have heard me, why didn't she wait?"

Fishwick was more concerned about Paul Butler standing by the airfield perimeter fence watching Maggie take off. "What's he up to? Better check him out."

Leaving Connie confused and still staring skyward, Fishwick walked purposely towards Mr. Butler to question him.

"Can I help you?" inquired Fishwick.

"Sorry must look a bit suspicious I know, let me explain." Said Butler.

Fishwick got the full story and did what he always did in times of awkward encounters – he took out his pipe and methodically packed and lit it.

"Could I ask you to watch out for her?" asked Mr Butler.

"I doubt if she will ever tell me but if she does then yes of course and she's got some very caring friends so there will be no shortage of support."

"Thank you." Said Butler with a distinct sadness in his voice. He strode off purposefully towards a 1930's MG salon car parked a few yards away.

Fishwick raised his hand to Butler as he drove off.

Maggie looked down through her tears at the green fields below. Just one push forward on the control stick and a steep dive into the ground from 6,000 feet would end her pain forever. She wouldn't feel a thing…ever again. "Yes, do it…fuck everything," she thought.

She leveled out and set course for Duxford.

A local village bus was making its way along a narrow country road. Joy was locked in conversation with a young schoolboy who was kneeling on the seat in front of Joy's to face her.

"Na, you don't fly Spitfires that's a pilot's job that is." said the boy.

"What do you think these are then clever clogs? Said joy as she tapped the wings on her tunic.

The youngster thought for a second then came back to her. "They're not proper wings are they? You're not a pilot. They might get you to clean the planes but you don't fly them…that's for men, that is."

"Cheek!" said Joy and started to laugh. The young boy joined in with the laughter.

The bus driver called out to Joy as the bus slowed down. "Your stop miss."

"Thank you," said Joy as she got up to leave. She turned to the boy as she picked up her bags from the overhead luggage rack. "Alright, next time you see a spitfire, wave and if it's me I'll wiggle the wings for you."

"You're on." Shouted the boy.

Still smiling Joy approached the gates of an airfield. Suddenly there was the sound of aero engines accompanied by a dark shadow cast over her. She looked up to see a huge American bomber filling the sky. She handed her papers to the military policeman on the gates. He checked them as he eyed Joy, who was still looking at the bomber disappearing into the distance. The MP lifted the barrier and Joy walked through to the US Army Air Force base.

It didn't take long for Joy to be engulfed in the American invasion of the English countryside. Americana was blasted at her from all angles. Apart from being wolf-whistled at by two very casually dressed airmen, the sound of loud jazz coming from an open window filled her head with sounds she'd never heard before.

A sharp "thwack" of a baseball bat hitting a ball was the next sound she heard followed by a deep Brooklyn accent calling out: "Strike one!"

A split second later there was a sound of breaking glass as the ball went through a nearby window "Ah shit." followed the same distant voice.

"Welcome to the United States," said Joy to herself.

After asking for directions from a bare-chested young airman on a bike, she arrived at a single- story building.
Joy handed her papers to a slightly overweight American officer and casually looked around at the various pictures and unfamiliar artifacts
that adorned the walls. A football helmet covered in signatures, a piece of torn fabric from a southern states flag signed pictures of Benny Goodman, Glen Miller and Charlie Parker and a framed collection of female film stars cigarette cards.

The officer's voice interrupted her fascination.

Officer: "But you're a girl."

Joy turned towards the officer, somewhat taken aback but was soon to respond.

"I can see why you're in a position of authority…you just can't be caught out can you darling? Was it the long hair or the lumps in the tunic?" said Joy with a bemused look.

"We are talking about a B-17 Fortress you know. They are a little heavier than what you may be used to." Continued the officer.

"Well I wasn't thinking of carrying it," said Joy with her hands on her hips like a precocious child, "more it carrying me was the plan."

The officer saw the funny side and began to warm to Joy.

"Come on," he said, "I'll walk with you, your limey engineer is already at the plane checking stuff over."

As they made their way across the airfield, acknowledged by various military personal flicking stylish salutes to the officer, he began to fill Joy in to what she could expect at her next destination.

"You're gonna find it pretty depressing over at Rivenhall, they're really getting a loser's deal. Long range daylight raids for the last three months. Horrendous casualties and a life expectancy to worry the crap out of a mayfly… if I was you I'd deliver this airborne coffin and get the hell out of it."

"Not the sort of place for a squeamish girl you mean?" commented Joy.

"It's not the sort of place for anyone in their right mind," answered the officer. "And there's no need to tear the ass out of the "girl" bit, you've proved your point."

"Nothing quite like rubbing it in though is there?" smiled Joy.

"Do you know what you've got?' said the officer.

"Please don't say spunk," said Joy cringing, "it means something totally different over here.

"I was going to say balls." Said the officer.

Joy climbed into the pilot's hatch of the bomber and called back. "I'll take that as a compliment then."

After about an hour of a cloudless sky Joy tuned her radio to Rivenhall tower and pressed the transmit button.

"Rivenhall this is alpha, tango alpha fortress, downwind for zero four."
"Tango alpha fortress, you're clear for zero four. Park left of active and we'll take her from there…and thanks for the delivery." Came the answer from the tower.

The Fortress touched down smoothly and parked. Joy got out followed by the flight engineer. A jeep pulled up beside the aircraft. "You carry," on said the flight engineer, "I've got a bit to do, see you later…get them to warm up a beer for me and I'll have one of those hamburger things."
Joy climbed into the jeep beside the young driver and slung her gear in the back.
Driving toward the distant buildings she saw evidence of what the officer had told her. Airmen sitting around with zombie like

expressions, a young airman leaning on a grass-covered bunker nervously tapping his foot to no evidence of music and several badly damaged aircraft; some completely burnt out.

Feeling the intense oppressive atmosphere Joy got out of the jeep as it arrived at the grey painted buildings and went into the reporting point with her papers. She handed them over to the desk sergeant. From outside she heard an argument taking place. She stepped to the open door and looked out. A young crew were sitting around an old gramophone player placed on a small flimsy chair.

One of the airmen was placing a record onto the turntable.

"I don't give a shit what you think, I like it and I'm playing it again."

A scratchy old Billie Holiday song started to play but didn't get very far.

Another airman jumped to his feet and kicked the gramophone player off the chair

As the gramophone player hit the floor, smashing the record, the perpetrator burst into a fit of rage. "That fucking record is getting on my tits."

As he went to sit back down his chair was kicked from beneath him causing him to fall flat on his back onto the grass. He sprang to his feet,

fist clenched, ready to throw a punch but stopped when he realised that the person who kicked the chair away was Joy. He stood staring at her for her moment, shaking still with fists tightly clenched.

Eventually Joy broke the silence. "You lot are in a ghastly mess aren't you?"
One of the airmen spoke up. "So would you be lady if you were sitting around waiting to die, which could be either this afternoon, tomorrow or maybe even next week if we really strike it lucky."

"Have you got a ball," said Joy.
"A what?" said the confused looking airman.
"A football," said Joy. "Not the funny shaped ones that you use but a proper one…a soccer ball."
Another young airman joined in. "Are you crazy?" He said.

"Well if you're all going to die what have you got to lose? Might as well have a bit of fun before you go.

"Frank's got a ball," came an answer from one of the airmen.

"Good…follow me." Said Joy.

One by one the confused looking airmen followed Joy across the field.

Joy called back as she made her way to an open area. "There's not enough of you, grab another couple of crews."

As the word went out Joy headed on her way like the pied piper. She stopped in the middle of the field and began to issue instructions to the now gathered twenty or so skeptical men.

"Right split into two teams then into pairs. For a start, you who kicked the gramophone over pair with you who's record it was."

The men shuffled around splitting up and pairing off, not knowing what they were doing or why.

Some distance away in a building overlooking the field the commanding officer and a junior officer were deep in, concerned, conversation. "It's really getting bad colonel," said the junior officer, "over the last couple of days it's almost reached flash point - they're beginning to fight each other."
The commanding officer spoke in an expressionless tone. "You know the situation lieutenant…so what's the answer?"

"Sir?" inquired the young officer.
The colonel continued. " I get the orders to bomb the hell out of Germany in broad daylight against German fighters and anti-

aircraft guns which means that crews don't come back…and the day after that I get another target and even more crews don't come back. And so it goes on and everyone is aware of the situation, including the crews that do get back and especially me lieutenant. So it figures by what you're saying that you've hit on a solution that I must have overlooked. So let's have it…lieutenant!"

"I don't have one sir," answered the somewhat embarrassed young officer, "I just thought that you should be aware of the situation."

The colonel barked back his response. "Don't ever…don't you damn well ever think that I'm not aware of guys, some of them eighteen years old in my command who are dying."

The officer attempted to offer a pathetic apology but didn't get very far. "Sir, I didn't mean…"

"Not ever lieutenant." Finished the colonel.

The sound of shouting interrupted the conversation. Loud shouting coming from across the field.

"Sounds like another fight." Said the lieutenant.

"Let's see this one for ourselves." Said the colonel.

They both stepped outside and were greeted by a bizarre sight. Half of Joy's entourage were wearing blindfolds and the other half were running alongside them shouting instructions to play football.

"What the hell is going on?" said the colonel. Two of the men, by their joint effort, manage to score a goal. The non-blindfolded man pulled the blindfold of his partner from his eyes to show him what they'd done and they both hug each other and jump up and down.

The colonel summoned one of the spectating ground crew over and asked:
"What is this?"
"We were all sitting round felling pretty pissed off sir when this angel flew down and things seemed to get a lot better." Said the airman.
Joy, who was by now wearing one of the crew's baseball caps, was refereeing the game.
The airman continued. "It's called blind man's soccer sir - it's great fun."

"Get me a scarf lieutenant," said the colonel.

"A what sir?" questioned the lieutenant.

"A blind fold man…and take off your jacket…we're playing." Said the colonel as he ran onto the makeshift pitch to rapturous applause from the non-blindfolded players. Their blindfolded partners pulled down their scarves then immediately joined in the applause to show their approval.

The colonel shouted to one of the men. "Hey Siano, pass the ball over here."

The colonel tied on his blindfold and turned to the lieutenant. "Shout at me lieutenant."

"Please kick now sir." Obeyed the lieutenant rather embarrassingly.

"Louder man." Barked the colonel. "Kick it…sir!" shouted the lieutenant.

The game carried on well into the afternoon, gathering more and more players until almost the whole of the base was either playing or cheering them on. Unknown to Joy, and drowned by the noise of the match, a radio was giving out an announcement in one of the now abandoned barrack blocks.

"The aviator Amy Johnson died earlier today after being reported missing in bad weather. Rescue attempts failed when she bailed out into the Thames estuary. Miss Johnson, famous for her pioneering solo flights, was serving with the Air Transport Auxiliary at the time of her death."

As dusk approached the game finally came to an end. The fun didn't though as the smell of burgers wafted across the airfield accompanied by the sound of beer cans being opened. Joy climbed into the open cockpit of an American trainer and tightened her harness. About a dozen or so of her new found friends had gathered to see her off including the colonel.

"You come back and see us soon and we'll teach you to play baseball." He said.
"We'll give the blindfold a miss with that one," smiled Joy, "could get a little dangerous."

The colonel stood to attention and saluted.
"Thanks for everything."

Joy climbed to three thousand feet and set course for White Waltham. With the slight tailwind she was due to arrive around 8.30pm and would still just be light. She would overfly the London docks then turn towards home. She smiled to herself as various jazz records continued to fill her head. A good day, she thought to herself proudly.

The engine of her aircraft gave out a slight splutter but cleared itself. Joy looked down at the instruments…all looked fine. She continued on for a few more miles.

Suddenly oil was sprayed over Joy's face. She coughed and spat. More oil splattered over her flying suit. Unable to see through the oil she ripped off her goggles and threw them away. At that moment the engine died.

"Mayday, mayday, mayday," she transmitted on her radio. "7804 Waco trainer engine failure. I'm about two miles south of London."

"Mayday 7804 Waco, I have you." Came a voice on the radio.

Joy pushed the stick forward so as not to stall and put the aircraft into a glide.
She looked over the side but could see nothing but cloud.
"Shit where's the ground?" she said to herself.

She slowly descended through the thick cloud. Straining her eyes to see the ground and hoping to get below the cloud base soon. All she could do was wait and keep her airspeed to a minimum to allow her as much time in the air as possible. As soon as she could see the ground she could select a place to land but all she could see was more and more cloud.

Eventually she broke free of the clouds and gave a sigh of relief as the ground became clear in front of her. But to her horror she saw that she was amongst a sky full of barrage balloons, protecting London from low flying enemy aircraft. She weaved around the anchor cables in a death defying slalom until one of the lethal cables of a barrage balloon ripped through her wing, severing it like a child's toy.

Joy's face was expressionless as if solemnly accepting the situation and realising that she was far too low for her parachute to have opened. She closed her eyes and waited for the inevitable to happen.

Final impact took a little longer than she expected.

Fishwick sat at his desk bolt upright. Maggie and Connie sat opposite him holding hands - a look of disbelief in their eyes.

"She did everything she could have done," explained Fishwick, She was just unlucky, just very unlucky. I'm not very good at this I'm afraid. I feel I should be saying things like: it was very quick and she didn't feel anything but I can't because I don't know. I don't really know what else to say, except…except I'm very sorry.

"Thank you, that will do," said Maggie softly.
"Will it?" Answered Fishwick. He reached for his pipe but pushed it away again.

Later that evening Maggie was lying on her bed, motionless, staring into space and holding her stork drawing. She turned her head toward Connie's room as she heard her crying. She so wanted to go and comfort her but just couldn't through fear of revealing her loss of John. A voice in her head was telling her to be strong. Was it her father's or Joseph's? She didn't know.

The early morning light broke through the makeshift curtains that didn't quite meet in the middle of Maggie's window. She was already dressed and brushing her hair. Completing her morning ritual she carefully placed the, now quite worn, stork drawing in her tunic pocket, took her bag from the hook on the back of the door and left. She could see Connie fast asleep through her slightly opened door. On the floor was a photograph of Joy posing by her first Tiger Moth, which Connie had taken. Maggie crept in, picked up the picture and placed it on the bedside table. Leaving the hut Maggie paused by the stork scoreboard. She took a pencil from her pocket and marked up Joy's last flight. She kissed her fingertips and touched Joy's name.

She walked slowly to the canteen, watching a young female new recruit being shown round by a senior officer. Inside she paid for a cup of tea and sat down at a table by the window. Fishwick joined Maggie at her table. Maggie gave a half smile to him and continued to watch the new recruit, clearly full of the moment and being as keen as was humanly possible.

After a few moments silence and still looking out of the window Maggie spoke.

"I bet she thinks it all sounds really attractive being able to fly any aircraft you can think of, and even getting paid for it…but how does she cope with the crap in between?"

Fishwick finished stirring his tea and tapped the spoon on the side of his cup as he looked toward the new recruit. "She copes with them in much the same way as she goes about her flying, because it's the only way she knows. When the weather closes in and things look bleak she sits it out and waits for the sky to get clearer, then she's up there again. There are times when the weather's rough for a long time and it really does get to her, but it can't rain forever. Then there are days when the sky is bright blue and everything is as clear as a bell and she can see for miles.

That's what keeps her going and why she keeps going and doesn't give up.

After another brief silence Maggie turned to Fishwick. "That beats the shit out of Churchill."

"Her sense of wit and sarcasm helps her to cope with life's pressures too of course." Said Fishwick raising his cup to his lips.

At that moment Maggie noticed Earnest driving toward the hut.
"Oh god I forgot about Earnest," said Maggie as she put down her half finished tea and ran to the door of the canteen.

By the time she got to the hut the familiar Rolls Royce was parked outside.

Maggie went inside and saw that Joy's door was open. She stood by the door and looked in. Earnest was by Joy's locker holding one of her silk scarves up to his face fondly. He turned to see Maggie in the doorway and quickly pushed the scarf into his pocket.

"Bloody typical isn't it?" said Earnest "Even when she's dead I'm clearing up after her."
"How are you Earnest?" Asked Maggie.
Earnest continued to throw things into a box with his back towards Maggie. Some things are thrown in slower as he took a little longer to look at them.
"Miss Joy was always quite decent to me really you know." He said carefully placing a selection of books into the box.

Maggie smiled as she walked round to Earnest's side trying to catch his eye.

"She wasn't too bad," he said as he held a pair of Joy's flying gloves tightly.

"Bit like having a daughter really."

Maggie reached out to touch Earnest but stepped back startled as Earnest hit Joy's locker hard with his fist.

"It's not bloody fair," he shouted.

Maggie stood frozen for a second then slung her arms around Earnest. They both began to cry. It first appeared to be Maggie comforting Earnest but then became the other way round as Maggie's crying became uncontrollable.

"You're not just crying for Miss Joy are you?" said Earnest

"Earnest I'm sorry." Wept Maggie

"I'm sure she wouldn't have minded," said Earnest, "especially as it's you…looked up to you she did."

"She wouldn't if she could see me now." Said Maggie.

"Want to talk about it?" asked Earnest.

"It doesn't seem fair on you." Said Maggie with her head now on Earnest's chest.

Earnest brushed the hair away from Maggie's face. "Remember I'm used to having a young lady to look after."

Earnest took Joy's scarf from his pocket and gave it to Maggie to wipe away her tears.

Fishwick was back in his office tidying his desk when Connie waked in.

"Reporting for duty Mr Fishwick. Sorry I'm a bit late, needed to go a bit of a walk to blow away the cobwebs." Said Connie forcing a smile.

"Nothing for you today." Answered Fishwick."

"What do you mean?" questioned Connie.

"Just as I said, nothing for you…relax, make the most of it."

"How come," said Connie, "has the war finished and no one told me? Or is a freak hurricane due to hit the whole of Britain in the next hour?"

"Neither as you well know." Continued Fishwick.

"Then why the hell can't I fly?" Connie argued.

Fishwick put his elbows on his desk, clenched both hands together and spoke looking Connie straight in the eye.

"Because in my opinion a valuable member of the Air Transport Auxiliary is temporarily indisposed…due to losing a very close friend and about seven hours sleep."

"Don't do this to me, please, I've got to work." Pleaded Connie.

"Good, said Fishwick, "You can work here, do a bit of that paperwork you always dump on me. There's enough of it to last the rest of the war."

He took a heavy looking file from a drawer and dropped it onto his desk in front of Connie.

"OK you win," said Connie.

Outside Fishwick's window Connie noticed Maggie giving Earnest a hand to load up the Rolls Royce with Joy's belongings.

"She's amazing isn't she," said Connie, "how does she do it?"

Fishwick walked over to the window filling his pipe. "I don't know, considering what she's been through lately."

"Sorry?" questioned Connie.

"Losing her young man of course." Answered Fishwick.

"What?" questioned Connie.

"The Army chap, couple of weeks ago."

Connie sat dumbstruck for a few seconds, then unknown to Fishwick who was still looking out of the window, went outside to join Maggie and Earnest. She took hold of one of the handles on a heavy bag that Maggie was struggling with.

"I can manage Con," said Maggie.

"Let me help, damn you," said Connie, Why didn't you tell me about him?"

"Who?" said Maggie sheepishly.

"I don't know who," shouted Connie, "because you never told me about him."

"God the world really is sneaking up on me today," said Maggie. "His name is…was John and you or no one knew about him because every time something good happens to me, fate has a nasty habit of whipping the rug from under my feet…I thought if I kept quiet about it this time I could avoid the fickle finger pointing in my direction…stupid really."

Connie took the bag off Maggie and put it into the Rolls Royce, before giving Maggie a lingering hug. "You do still have the best friend a girl could have you know."

"Thanks Con," smiled Maggie. "Now that's enough of the huggy American shit."

Chapter ten
Up with me

Fishwick's secretary, Janet was standing in the open doorway to her boss's office with her hand covering the mouthpiece of a telephone. "Sir, it's the commanding officer from the American airbase at Rivenhall; colonel Martin." "Put him through," answered Fishwick in a resigned tone, "what's the betting it's a complaint about one of the clowns from our circus flying?"

Fishwick picked up the phone and waited for the worse. "Fishwick, good morning Colonel." After a few seconds a look of confusion came across his face followed by the slightest hint of a smile. In the next room Janet, who was listening in, wiped a tear from the corner of her eye.

"Thank you Colonel," said Fishwick, "yes she's very sadly missed."
Fishwick continued to listen, as did Janet who was now putting her hand to her mouth to try not to laugh.
"She did what?" said Fishwick. "I suppose it was pretty typical of her come to think of it. No she didn't make a habit of playing blind

man's football on a regular basis, not to my knowledge but she was a bit of an 'on the spur of the moment' kind of person and a little impetuous at times."

Both Fishwick and Janet continued to listen as the colonel continued his main reason for the call. "We kind of feel we owe her one," said the Colonel, "so if it's OK with you we'd like to make a little presentation to the appropriate family and friends and relatives. If you would kindly
send me a list? Oh and could you send me a picture of Joy please? All will be revealed why we need it"

"I would be pleased to do that," agreed Fishwick. "May I suggest that the presentation is in, let's say, a couple of months time? I think all concerned will be in a better frame of mind to appreciate the occasion."

"Agreed." Said Colonel Martin.

Janet stepped into the room as soon as the phones were put down.
"I think Maggie and Connie should definitely be on the list sir."
"What list would that be?" Inquired Fishwick
Realising that she had been caught out somewhat, Janet tried to cover up. "Er I thought it best to stay on the line in case there were notes to be taken Mr.
Fishwick…especially as he is a Colonel in the allied forces so to speak."

"Ever considered a future in the Diplomatic Service?" Asked Fishwick

"Sir?" inquired a confused Janet.

"Never mind," said Fishwick, "and yes I had considered Miss Stewart and Miss Macovich to be included thank you. Maybe you should inform them…if you haven't already of course."

"Of course I haven't sir, wouldn't be so forward."

"Then be my guest," suggested Fishwick, "and make sure they realise this applies only if there isn't a call for any urgent deliveries. The war comes first…as always. Time for a cuppa I feel Janet." Fishwick was proved right, as usual, as the next two months passed and winter was

beginning to be felt in the morning air. Joys death was far from forgotten and still brought a tear to the two remaining friends eyes but the reality and acceptance of what happened seemed to bring them closer together. Even Maggie began to confide in Connie on occasions and Connie, in turn, was able to share fond memories of her childhood with Bob with a smile that acknowledged her distinctive, natural beauty.

Familiar faces gathered and mingled in the small anteroom at Rivenhall air base. Joy's parents, Diana and Richard Bamforth, Maggie, Connie, Fishwick, Romek, Jimmy and of course Ernest, who had distanced himself from everyone else and was eagerly trying as many canapés and cocktails as he could before the presentation took place. The content of which was still to be revealed to all.

The Bamforths were talking to Connie and Romek.

"Joy told us you're Polish," Said Diana, "We had a delightful month in Gdansk a few years ago - beautiful little hotel by the river. What part of Poland are you from?"

"New York," answered Connie with a cheeky smile.

"Oh do they have one too? Said Diana.

"I think Connie means the one in America darling." Said Richard.

"Actually my folks come from Warsaw Mrs Bamforth," continued Connie, "but the nearest I've ever been to Poland is about where I'm standing now…more of a yank than a Pole." "I know Gdansk very well," said Romek, "and so will Connie when the war is over and she allows me to take her there. It's about time she had her roots re-potted. You must give me the name of that hotel."

At the other end of the room Fishwick was talking to Colonel Martin.
"Ok, I think it's time." Said the colonel.
Fishwick assisted the colonel by tapping on his glass to attract attention from the room.

The colonel announced: "Ladies and gentlemen, if I could have your attention please.
First of all, on behalf of the whole of the base and three, nine, seven group, I'd like to welcome you to Rivenhall. As you all know, the purpose of today is a presentation in recognition of your very dear Joy Bamforth who left a lasting impression on the crews of

this base. The only slight problem is that this presentation is a little too large to fit inside this room, so if you will all kindly follow me outside, and apologies in advance for your severe climate, all will be revealed."

With a mixture of excitement and intrigue the assembled guests shuffled outside into the cold late morning air. The sky was clear making it feel even chillier.

Following close behind the colonel, after a five-minute walk, they arrived at a large hanger. Outside there was a small roped off area and either side of the hanger doors was a guard in full dress uniform. A collection of military musicians, some rubbing their hands to keep them warm, were waiting for their cue.

The colonel gestured for the guests to take their place inside the roped off area and began to make his speech.

"Well here we are, not too cold for you I hope." He paused, a little nervously for a second then continued. "You never quite know if these things are going to be appropriate but it was the only thing we could think of. In the very short time that we knew Joy, she managed to breath new life into this unit and so we wanted to do something to recognise this but also to do something that we think Joy would have wanted and I think you will agree that was to carry on flying. So that's exactly what we've done."

Maggie and Connie looked at each other puzzled, at which point the band struck up with "Coming in on a wing and a prayer" as the hanger doors opened. A Marauder bomber was towed out of the hanger, revealing something that brought an instant smile to some of the guest's lips.

On the side of the aircraft was a freshly painted emblem. A reasonable likeness of Joy wearing a very skimpy version of her ATA uniform with the words "Joy to life" lettered around her. A truly British hush fell over the audience as the band finished their piece. The colonel looked around nervously. Then slowly and contagiously the applause grew to quite a raucous level. Relieved and pleased with the reaction the colonel signaled to the band to strike up again.

Earnest stepped forward and looked up at the painting.

"She would have liked that." He said. "She would have liked those too." Said Connie as both she and Maggie were somewhat distracted by the size of chest that the enthusiastic artist had given Joy.

Colonel Martin felt a tap on his shoulder. He turned to see Earnest who whispered something into his ear. The Colonel smiled and nodded. He led Earnest to the pilot's hatch of the aircraft. Connie noticed what was happening and informed Maggie. "What's the old fox up to Mags? She said. "Don't know but nothing would surprise me." Answered Maggie.

The colonel returned to his guests without Earnest. After a few seconds the aircraft's propellers burst into life drowning the sound of the band. The small crowd turned to see the bomber slowly move forward. High above them, seated next to the pilot was Earnest looking a little ridiculous in a leather-flying helmet. There was a huge, schoolboy, grin on his face. The bomber taxied to the runway, put on full power and took off into the clear blue sky.

It roared overhead to another round of applause from the small gathering below. Gazing up, Diana Bamforth turned to her husband and said. "Looks like they're off again then."
Richard smiled, put his arm around her shoulder and gave a little wave to the bomber, which had become a tiny speck in the sky.

Chapter 11
Final fling

The days went by, as did the weeks, recorded by the stork scoreboard now looking very full. Both Maggie's and Connie's entries had long overtaken Joy's last tragic flight, which was lovingly preserved with two kisses in Joy's favourite lipstick alongside it.

The daily routine had somewhat changed from delivering Spitfires and Hurricane fighters to ferrying two and four engine bombers and transport planes, most of which had the D-Day stripes painted clearly on their wings. But it was no less busy. Flights were mostly long distance and more exhausting. There was even the occasional delivery to France, Belgium or Norway, often ending with a boat and rail trip back. This gave the two young women a new insight into war; traveling alongside wounded soldiers, sailors and airmen was a far cry from the bird's eye view that they had been used to.

On one of these journeys back to England Maggie was to experience something beyond her wildest imaginings. After delivering a repaired Dakota to a small makeshift airfield in Normandy she hitched a ride in a US jeep to the port of Dieppe. As she handed her papers to a military policeman, and asked permission to board a ship, he warned her. "This isn't going to be a pleasure cruise Miss.

The whole deck is strewn with casualties, some of them not a pretty sight…could be a bit upsetting."

Although partially grateful for the advice Maggie was also somewhat annoyed at the policeman's view on her ability to cope with the situation. She stuffed her papers into her tunic pocket and strode up the gangway to board the ship. "Thank you corporal, maybe a woman's touch will come in handy."

What she was greeted with was no exaggeration by the policeman; pathetic figures on stretchers covered in blood, missing limbs and many of them writhing in agony. Maggie became paralyzed at the horror she was confronted with. Her motionless gaze was disturbed by a frantic voice of a medic's carrying one end of a stretcher. "Out the way lady." As the second stretcher bearer passed Maggie she asked, "Is there anything I can do to help?" "Do what you can, where you can Miss, that's all we're doing." She saw another young medic laden with first aid bags and a bucket of water. "Let me help," pleaded Maggie. "Take this and follow me," replied the medic as he gave Maggie the water. He led her to the other side of the ship just as it started to leave the port. "We've done everything we can for this lot so just give them some water." Said the medic as he left Maggie to it. Maggie could see that some of the men were not going to make the journey home; others were propped up against the ship's railings with cigarettes in their mouths. Maggie began by giving water to those who were conscious enough to drink and wetting the lips of those who weren't.

As she was holding a young Royal Marine's head up to drink she heard a voice.
"Helft mir bitte."
Maggie looked round, startled to hear a German voice. A middle-aged sergeant with a bandaged head, sitting on a wooden crate explained. "He's a Jerry Miss, he was so messed up and covered in blood they couldn't even recognize his uniform…thought he was French or something. Don't think the poor bugger's going to make it…only got half his guts left"

Maggie knelt down beside the young German.
"Ich bin hier, ich werde dir helfen."

The German soldier reached out his hand towards Maggie.

"Das ist mein Freida?"

Without a moments hesitation Maggie held the young German's hand and became his Freida.

"Ja, es ist ich, Ihre Freida."

The German soldier smiled as best he could and whispered, "Ich liebe dich Freida."

Maggie didn't know the young man's name but replied in the only way she could think of.

"Ich liebe dich auch mein Schatz." (I love you too sweetheart)

The young man's grip on Maggie's hand tightened for just a few seconds then loosened and went cold. It was if he was hanging on for this moment. "Can't think of a better way to go," said the sergeant, "even though he was a

Jerry." Maggie didn't answer; she just held the dead soldier's hand for a little while longer then carried on giving the other injured men water.

On her return to the airfield Maggie didn't tell Connie about the young German, she wasn't sure herself why she didn't tell her. She wanted to believe that it was because Connie shouldn't be subjected to any more stories of death but deep down she feared that Connie would question how she could show such compassion to the enemy – the enemy that killed her brother.

During this time the sky was continually filled with aircraft like bees delivering their nectar to the hive - the accompanying sound of aero engines ever present throughout the day and night became perfectly normal.

'Joy to life' managed to survive against the terrible odds endured by the US Army Air Force's daylight bombing raids. The painting of joy became a little more faded and was now surrounded by symbols of bombs marking numerous successful missions.

Paul and Fiona Butler visited their local churchyard every day where their son John was laid to rest. Early one evening, as they walked toward the church, they saw a shadowy figure of what looked like a young woman leaving the graveyard. They arrived at the grave and saw that a fresh bunch of wild flowers had been placed under the headstone. They didn't see their own Rolls Royce, which was parked at the back of the church leave with Earnest at the wheel and Maggie in the back seat.

Earnest, in fact, had become a regular visitor to the airfield, chauffeuring Connie and Maggie to the railway station and occasional nights out to the local pub. Without showing any signs of admitting it, he had grown very fond of them and it enabled him to regain what he missed so much… moaning for being kept waiting and running around after young women. He also, when no one was looking, dusted and made sure there were no spiders in Joy's old room, which Connie and Maggie had persuaded Fishwick to leave unoccupied.

Quite slowly, like the transformation to a new season, things started to change. Almost unrealised the skies became quieter. Like a mischievous hand slowly turning down the volume of a radio that went unnoticed until there was no sound at all. At least the sound of a war that had been so dominant over the years wasn't there. Instead a new music had taken over – its musicians being a dog barking, birds singing and the occasional car horn as it announced its presence along a winding country lane.

By now the old stork scoreboard had an extension nailed onto the bottom of it, recording every flight, aircraft and adventure that Connie and Maggie had had since Joy's final entry.

They sat either side of it in two non-matching deckchairs. Maggie carefully folded a piece of paper into an aeroplane and threw it into the air. It dived and crashed to the ground beside a dozen or so other failed attempts.

"I appreciated the rest for the first couple of days," said Connie.
"How long's it been now?" asked Maggie tearing another piece of paper out of an old notebook.
"One week two and a half days," answered Connie.
"I'd even settle for a Tiger Moth." Said Maggie.
"I'd fight you for it." Said Connie.

A young airman cycled up to them and circled round saying: "Fishface wants to see you two layabouts."

Connie commented as Maggie threw the last paper aeroplane at the airman.

"He's a charmer isn't he?"

Inside his office Fishwick was pouring himself a coffee. He pointed to two cups as the women entered offering them one for the first time ever. Connie accepted and held out her cup.

"You've probably noticed that things have been slowing down lately…they seem to be coping well enough without us these days. We may well be disbanded soon although I haven't had any official word yet." Informed Fishwick.

He slid a couple of documents towards the women.

"So this looks like your last one…good news is, it's twins. Latest mark Spitfires with all mod cons. There's one for North Weald and one for Biggin Hill."

Connie was quick to comment; "I'll take the one for North Weald if that's OK?"

"I thought you might," said Fishwick. "Only thing is some gormless twit has gone and fueled them full to the brim…so you'll have to burn quite a bit off. Don't want to go landing on full tanks as well you know."

The familiar smile known to light up Connie's face returned as she turned to leave the office. Maggie glanced back at Fishwick and detected a hint of a smile in return.

Fishwick called after them as they left; "Just one more thing?" "Sir?" answered Connie. "Did you ever decide on a nickname? Just curious you understand."

"No sir we didn't." answered Maggie."

"Very well," said Fishwick, "have a good flight."

The two women linked arms as they made their way to the brand new waiting Spitfires.

"I didn't have the heart to tell him." Said Maggie

"Me neither," agreed Connie. "He turned out OK. What are you going to do when it's over Mags?"

"Try and look up Joseph and Maria if they're still around and if they still want to know me. Then, I don't know…I hear there's a shortage of crop sprayers in Canada…fancy it?"

"Sure, sound great," said Connie. Maggie detected a little uncertainty in Connie's voice and smiled to herself.

They arrived at their last babies and handed over the papers to a waiting mechanic. "Don't know why old Fishbone wanted these fueled full you're only going round the corner so to speak." He said.

Maggie and Connie gave each other a knowing look before doing the usual walk-around safety checks. Maggie climbed into the cockpit as Connie stood back to take a few pictures.

Side by side the two Spitfires took off in perfect synchrony.

"How about we give a fond farewell to Mackerel?" said Maggie on the intercom.
"Crazy not to," replied Connie.

The Spitfires approached the airfield building on a less than treetop height at full power. Inside his office Fishwick was, as usual, lighting his pipe. There was a tremendous roar from the two Rolls Royce Merlin engines as they flew overhead.
Fishwick's first reaction was to duck and then to laugh out loud quite hysterically and completely out of character. Unknown to Fishwick his laughter was joined by Connie's and Maggie's as they climbed away into a bright blue sky.

"Better burn some of that fuel off then Con." Said Maggie.

"Do you think we have to burn it off the right way up?" Answered Connie.

"Nothing in any rule book to say why we should," Maggie replied. The local primary school was just finishing for the day. The sound of the
aircraft caused a small group of children to look up and be treated to free air show.
There was a dialogue in the sky. Every aerobatic maneuver made by each aircraft was answered by the other. A visual symphony of loops, rolls, spins and turns made more people stop to look up.

The school bus arrived and the middle aged driver got out to take a better look.
He smiled as he said to a waiting parent; "that's why we won the Battle of Britain…those boys can really fly.

"I don't think we can stretch it out for much longer." Said Maggie "come on I'll see you to North Weald."

Connie landed and slid back her canopy. As she looked around at the familiar surroundings, Maggie flew overhead, waved her wings and then headed off towards her final destination. Connie switched off her engine and softly mouthed; "bye Mags."

Connie ran her fingers over the instrument panel and placed her other hand on the control column. She tapped it affectionately as she breathed in the familiar smells of leather, metal and fuel. It was just as she had remembered it; nothing had changed except ten years had passed.

A young airman leaned into the cockpit from the outside. "Bring back any memories mam?"

"Oh yes said Connie…heaps."

Beside the Spitfire was a small Air Transport Auxiliary exhibition display stand featuring a collection of Connie's old photos of the aircraft that she had religiously photographed during her time in the ATA.

She climbed out of the Spitfire to join Romak who was holding a baby girl in one arm and holding another little boy's hand with his other hand.

The annual White Waltham Airshow was enjoying a good turn out.

"Feel better now?" asked Romak.

Connie smiled; "yeah that should last me for a couple of years."

As the young family went to walk away Connie glanced back for a final look.

"I don't believe it…Just a second." Said Connie to Romak.
She went back to the display stand and tapped a smartly dressed elderly man on the shoulder, who was looking at the Connie's old photographs.

"Hello Mr Fishwick"
Fishwick turned round. The distinctive thin moustache had gone and what hair he had left was now completely white. The only clue to suggest that he used to be a man in uniform was his highly polished shoes.

"Good afternoon Miss Kletzi." Said Fishwick, as formal as ever.

"Actually the name's Janowski now," said Connie.

Romak and the Children appeared on the scene. Romak handed over the baby girl to Connie and grabbed Fiskwick's hand and shook it vigorously.

"Mr Fishwick, how wonderful to see you." Fishwick was a little taken aback by Romak's burst of affection.

"Ah, Romak isn't it? Yes, splendid looking family you have. And what's your name young man? Said Fishwick to the little boy.

"Bob," said the boy shyly.

Fishwick, smiled at Connie. "And this young lady." Continued Fishwick pointing to the baby girl.

"This is Diza," replied Connie.

"What a charming name" said Fishwick.

"It's Hebrew meaning Joy." Said Connie.

Fishwick nodded continuously. "Perfect, perfect. Ever hear from that friend of yours…what was her name?"

"You know darn well it's Maggie," replied Connie cheekily. "I think you had a bit of a crush on her."

Fishwick laughed "no, no no!"

"We write to each other, well I do most of the writing. She's in Canada, still flying and running a small freight business. She went back to Germany about a year after the war to discover that Joseph and Maria had been killed in a bombing raid on the airfield."

"How very sad." Said Fishwick.

"Yes" replied Connie, "very sad."

" Well I suppose we'd better be going, lovely to see you Mr Fishwick."

Connie hesitated for a moment then kissed Fishwick on the cheek.

"And thank you for everything."

"My pleasure." Fishwick smiled.

Connie gave Diza a hug and said. "Come on, Mummy's had her fun, let's go home."

As they all climbed into the Ford Prefect the little boy asked; "where did you used to sleep Mummy?"

Connie smiled "oh that's all gone now honey…gone and all forgotten."

In a disused corner of the airfield two workmen were demolishing some old buildings overgrown with weeds and blackberry bushes that had been allowed to flourish during the years that had passed. One of the workmen pulled what was left of the old stork scoreboard from the undergrowth.

"What do you think this is?"

The other workman merely glanced at it; "Dunno, some kid's thing maybe…chuck it on the fire."

As the Janowski's car left the airfield familiar words echoed back to Connie.

>*Up with me! up with me into the clouds!*
>*For thy song, Lark, is strong;*
>*Up with me, up with me into the clouds!*
>*Singing, singing,*
>*With clouds and sky about thee ringing,*
>*Lift me, guide me till I find*
>*That spot which seems so to thy mind!"*

Printed in Great Britain
by Amazon